You Must Fight Them

YOU MUST FIGHT THEM

A Novella and Stories

Maceo Montoya

UNIVERSITY OF NEW MEXICO PRESS • ALBUQUERQUE

Library of Congress Cataloging-in-Publication Data
Montoya, Maceo.
    [Short stories. Selections]
    You must fight them : a novella and stories / Maceo Montoya. — First
edition.
        pages ; cm
    ISBN 978-0-8263-4199-0 (softcover : acid-free paper) —
    ISBN 978-0-8263-4589-9 (electronic)
    I. Title.
    PS3613.O54945A6 2015
    813'.6—dc23
                                2014046090

"The Stuttering Roommate" was previously published in *Eleven
Eleven*; "How I Broke Up with the Mayor" was previously published
in *Huizache*.

Cover painting *Cielo Rojo XVII*, 2010, charcoal and acrylic on paper,
22" x 30", by Maceo Montoya. Interior painting *Conozco bien los últi-
mos vislumbres de tantos atardeceres*, 2009, acrylic on canvas,
23" x 18", by Maceo Montoya. Both paintings were previously published in *Letters to the Poet from His Brother* (Copilot Press, 2014).
Book design by Catherine Leonardo
Composed in Melior LT Std Roman
Display font is ITC Kabel Std.

for 1305½ Fremont Street

Contents

—ɯ—

You Must Fight Them

A Novella

—ɯ—

for Ricky Salinas

CHAPTER ONE

I

I FIRST SAW Lupita Valdez in junior high. At the time I was barely four foot eleven. I was chubby and wore glasses. To make matters worse I had a shock of thick, wavy hair, which I tried taming with pink globs of L.A. Looks. By fourth period the globs would dry and start to flake. I looked like I'd been flocked. To this day I wonder why my parents didn't say something; they imparted plenty of lessons, but hair-gel application was not one of them. Lupita and I were in science together and she sat next to me, but a table over. I remember she wore a Raiders jersey. She already wore makeup and large hoop earrings, and I could always smell her fruity perfume, or maybe it was just her lotion. Whatever it was, she doused herself in it and the smell made me light headed. But it was also her presence that overwhelmed me. Of course, I had no words for these feelings; I was more focused on basketball at lunchtime, but I knew what it was like to feel her next to me, to know that one glance in my direction was enough to make my ears burn—my cheeks too, I couldn't help it—and it would only worsen when others noticed. "Look at heeem," they would screech. "Look how red he is! Why you so red?" And Lupita would pretend to ignore them, pretend not to have noticed, and I was grateful, but I was also confused. What mercy did she owe me? She'd turn back to her book as if she'd glanced in my direction only by accident, to fix her hair, to stare out the window, to merely look past me across the room at someone else.

Only once did she address me, and even though she swears she spoke to me more—she remembers asking me for help all the time—I know without a doubt that it was only once. She asked me something about the moon and gravity, its relationship to high and low tides, though she stated this more crudely, of course. I turned to her, feeling my face burning, but I must

3

not have turned as red as usual because no one took notice, or at least they kept quiet. I quickly looked away (and as a result I have no memory of her face, maybe just her smile), and I turned to my book and pointed to the answer, unable to say it aloud. She thanked me and that was it.

She was the most beautiful girl in my grade, in my school, and she always would be. Her family had moved to Woodland from someplace else, Fairfield I remember hearing, but it was actually Vallejo. They said the family had to leave because of her, because she had developed a bad reputation. How do seventh graders know so much? How do they know what rumors to spread? Where does their sudden bloodthirsty viciousness come from? To this day I see boys and girls of that age and I imagine the worst of them. I know what they're capable of. It's as if we're born with it, the desire to destroy one another; it lies latent for a time and then it emerges, full force, at twelve. They called her a slut. They said that she was run out of her previous school. "Why? Why?" the little brats chorused. "Cuz she fucked hella dudes, that's why." I never believed it. I didn't think it possible. Because even then I was a hopeless romantic. I was also sheltered; such vulgar language made me squirm. I was fed plenty of books, but adolescent pastimes like video games, television, R-rated movies, and afternoons spent shooting the shit behind the school grounds—all those were off limits. I was on the cusp of puberty, but I possessed the street wisdom of a six-year-old. I believed in purity. What did that mean to a seventh grader? I don't recall. What does it even mean now? Purity! All I know is that I believed in hers. She was beautiful, she was good, and she smelled like vanilla and peaches. The rumors disappeared eventually, sometimes still whispered, I'm sure, but mostly they were forgotten. I, who never believed them, never forgot.

Every now and then I would hear of her brothers. The Valdez brothers, branded like outlaws. I heard they were Norteño gangbangers and they only fought together, all three of them back to back, except when one of them was in juvenile hall for tagging or stealing or violating his probation, and then they fought as two. It was in my freshman year that I first learned

4

that in order to date Lupita Valdez you had to fight them, one against three. At the time, I knew of only one who'd dared so far, a Norteño from Dixon, an eighteen-year-old. People said he was big. In my mind he had to be a Goliath. His name was Willie, but everyone called him Spider. I tried to imagine a giant hairy spider fighting off three cholos. Then I tried to imagine that same spider arm in arm with Lupita. I heard he ended up in jail. Later, I learned of others who took the challenge, all of them Norteños, friends of her brothers, but some said they just fought to *try* and be with her. It was no guarantee you'd end up dating. Meaning, you fought for the chance. Guys cursed this barrier, this impossible obstacle. More than once I overheard someone say, "Man, I'd talk to her any day of the week, I don't even care, but her brothers . . . *fuck*," and with that *fuck* all would be understood. Girls claimed that Lupita herself put her brothers up to it; they said that the stuck-up bitch thought she was worth dying for. More than a few vatos thought that she was. I thought it all very terrifying.

In between my junior and senior year of high school I had to take summer school PE in order to make room for all honors classes my senior year. Thinking I could possibly add muscle mass to my thin frame (I'd lost my baby fat thanks to a growth spurt in the ninth grade), I took weight lifting. Lupita Valdez was in my class period, but she and her friends chose badminton. Before class we had to line up for roll call, the girls against one wall, the guys across the room against the other. As it happened, my last name and hers corresponded so that we sat directly across from one another. She had been dating someone for a while, the only guy I could imagine her with. His name was Ernesto Rocha, but everyone called him Ernie. He was six foot, already built like a man. He looked as if he had emerged from the womb with a full goatee. He didn't claim blue or red, but he dressed the part: perfectly pressed Dickies, white T-shirts, Pendletons buttoned only at the top, a khaki belt with the strap hanging down to his knees, and steel-toed boots. In high school the rubric seemed to go like this: to be Mexican was to be tough, and the tougher you were the more Mexican you were. Which is to say, Ernie Rocha was Pancho Villa, Emiliano Zapata, and Julio César Chávez rolled into the tricolor flag. I heard that he fought the Valdez brothers with no one around, and that they'd arranged it that way because they were afraid he'd get the best of them. Others said that they'd agreed to forgo the fight altogether. No one ever saw Ernie with so much as a scratch or bruise.

Everyone respected Ernie. Treated him with adulation is more like it, even the teachers who loved that he called them sir and ma'am without a hint of facetiousness. But I must have admired him most of all. Sure, I daydreamed about karate chopping a gangbanger from time to time, the straight-A student as closeted vato loco, but my respect wasn't for his physical prowess. Rather, I needed to know what it was that he possessed: the calm demeanor of someone who knows he's capable of handling whatever comes his way. He was feared, not because he did anything to cause fear, but merely because he appeared to be tougher than anyone else, and this without ever having to prove it. Like his fight with the Valdez brothers: maybe he fought them, maybe he didn't. What mattered was he ended up with Lupita without seeming to have suffered the least bit of pain.

My reverence for Ernie, however, stemmed from a specific encounter in my sophomore year. At this point I should probably mention that my father is Chicano and my mother is white. Simple enough. As genes would have it, I can pass for white: light-brown hair, brown eyes with flecks of hazel, and skin that burns after ten minutes in the sun. My father, however, a professor of ethnic studies at the community college, would never allow that. To him nothing was more important than your history and culture. My mother felt less strongly about this issue; maybe she's more Swedish than English, and she's also kind of Irish, I guess, and there's probably some German in there too, but did she really have claim to any of these? Well, my entire freshman year my father hounded me about joining the Mestizo Club. He was asked to give a lecture to the group about the Chicano Movement, and he thought his dutiful son would be in attendance, but I didn't go. I didn't

6

want to. I had already dealt too often with the explanations, the repeated insistence, "I'm not white, I'm Chicano. My father is Mexican, I swear. Just look at my last name!" And they'd say, "That's like Italian or some shit." In junior high I even tried to wear baggy khakis sagged halfway down my ass, but my mother only bought me Dockers and it just doesn't look the same. I tried to wear the white T-shirts with the black-and-white lowrider designs or the indigenous warriors holding half-naked princesses, but always someone would say, "Why *you* wearing that?" as if I had trespassed on some unspoken boundary. So I gave up, for the most part. I had friends who were Mexican (Tony Galíndez foremost among them), who accepted me as some amalgamation of themselves, but unfortunately as my classes went in a different direction— the honors English and history, the advanced-placement track—I had less and less contact with them.

My father and I argued about the Mestizo Club for months. I would tell him, "Dad, the club's motto is 'Pride for My Race.' Do I look like I'm part of that race?" And he, golden-skinned with a thick black mustache, would respond, "La Raza means so much more than that; it's not just about skin tone. I grew up in the fields, your grandfather was a bracero! That's part of you, mijo!" He couldn't place himself in my shoes, couldn't imagine how ridiculous it felt to be in a room full of brown kids and insisting you were one of them. To him it was a state of mind. My culture was a part of me whether I recognized it or not. I chose what I embraced, not others. Our arguments often ended with me yelling at him, "It's very simple, Dad: if you wanted a Mexican son you shouldn't have married a white woman!" And my mom would chime in, "Hey there, now, sweetheart." Eventually he wore me down. I promised him I'd at least try to attend a meeting.

So one day I went, a Thursday right after school, and I entered Mrs. Thompson's Spanish classroom and was met with what I perceived as a few confused stares. I also got some hard looks from a few vatos, but in truth they looked at everyone that way. I was suddenly conscious that I was wearing a sweater-vest. Could I have picked something more conspicuous? I sat in the corner waiting for Mrs. Thompson to show up, the club advisor. People carried on with their conversations. I was ignored. I scanned the room, looking for a friendly face. Lupita was there, but except for a brief glance when her head was turned I avoided looking in her direction. The last thing I wanted to do was turn bright red. There was another girl, a friend of hers named Mary, whom I'd long had a crush on. We were friends, and I thought maybe she'd say hello. I kept staring in her direction, hoping she'd turn my way, but she ignored me, along with everyone else. Which was fine; I actually preferred to remain unnoticed in the corner, closest to the door. Maybe I could slip out at some point. I settled for staring at a conjugation chart of irregular verbs. Then Abel Castro, his face marred with pimples, walked in the room, opening the heavy glass door wildly so that it slammed against the doorstop. He met my eyes, briefly looked down (possibly at my sweater-vest), and said, obnoxiously loud and with a smirk, "What are *you* doing here?"

Normally, I wouldn't have cared what Abel Castro had to say. He was always overly dramatic, and anyway he may have been genuinely curious to know what I was doing there. But now I felt as if the entire room had turned to stare at me and was awaiting my answer. My ears were burning. "I'm here for the meeting," I managed to say.

He snorted, but before he could say anything else, whatever it might have been, Ernie Rocha appeared in the doorframe, wearing a perfectly pressed long white T-shirt. He was alone. He never walked with a following like the others; he was always a solitary figure, and this added to his stature. Everyone else was so in need of others' approval that to walk alone meant you lacked it, but not him. He was wearing Lokes, the dark shades every cholo wore, and after briefly assessing the room he removed them and hung them ever so smoothly in the collar of his shirt. He walked in and without greeting anyone else he looked at me and said, "Yo, I know your pops, he came and talked to us last year." I can't remember if I responded or not. I must have. Maybe I just smiled dumbly, flattered that he knew who I was. He came over and shook my hand in the overly complicated way that some Chicanos do—I can't describe it exactly, but it involves at least three motions and can end knuckles to knuckles or with a half embrace, which always catches me off guard, but I must've done it correctly because we pounded each other's fists like old friends—and that was all I needed to be accepted that day. After that, even though I only went to a couple more meetings, I felt as if my presence was never again questioned. It was also, I remember, when I started referring to my friends' fathers as "your pops," but I dropped it after a couple of months when Tony Galíndez told me it just sounded weird coming out of my mouth.

So Lupita was Ernie Rocha's girl and it made sense. In my world scheme, he was the only one who could be with her. But there she was, summer school PE, sitting directly across from me in the roll-call line, to the left of Frederica Vasquez and Paula Zamora. We wore the same clothes: a gray T-shirt that said Wolves PE, and black sweat shorts, our names written in Sharpie marker. And every morning I would stare at my shoes, or the floor, or the weight equipment, and I would wonder what the hell I was doing there, wasting my summer so that I could make room for one more honors class, one more class to boost my GPA, all so that I could be valedictorian and go to school on the East Coast and get as far away from this hick farm town as possible. Sometimes I would look across the room at the row of girls and I'd look at their legs, so many shades of brown (a few pale ones). I'd wonder what each of them looked like naked, and I would imagine a world with no clothes, but I wouldn't dwell too long, afraid of an inopportune erection. Also, I would feel guilty, as if somehow my fantasy alone had degraded them (my parents never spoke to me about sex, but they talked plenty about not objectifying women). So I would scan their faces and wonder what they would be like when they were older, which ones would grow ugly, which ones would grow fat (this objectification rested easier with me), and I'd wonder if they stared

9

across the room assessing the guys in the same way. Then one day as I scanned the faces of the row of girls, I found a set of eyes staring in my direction. Surprised to find someone returning my gaze, I didn't look away, as if I were stunned. I kept looking directly at her, wondering, wondering why Lupita Valdez was staring at me. Then she smiled and looked away. The first time it happened I was sure I'd been mistaken.

The second time I thought there must be something she found funny, and I became self-conscious wondering what it could be. I must have turned shades of red, because she looked away, flushed as well. When we were excused I went to the bathroom and looked in the mirror. There was nothing different about me. I looked the same as I always did: my narrow face surrounded by wavy brown hair somewhat tamed with gel, now wearing contacts instead of glasses, and slightly less pale because it was summer. The next day, however, I knew there'd been no mistake. I scanned the row of girls as Mr. Fracaso, in his orange-and-black warm-up suit, called out their names. One by one they responded, "Here!" in their chirpy voices, and my eyes passed over them. Then two guys on my side of the room started play-fighting, and one of them hurled the other against the weight bench. He grabbed his leg in exaggerated pain, then lunged to kick his friend. The commotion distracted Mr. Fracaso. He set down his clipboard and rushed across the room, limping because his left leg was lame, thinking it was a real fight, calling out, "Now, now, none of that!" And everyone thought this was hilarious, especially the two kids fighting. I laughed with the others, but I wasn't really paying attention. I could hear Mr. Fracaso lecturing us, but I was thinking to myself, *What if I turned right now, what if I turned, would she be looking?* And I turned, and sure enough our eyes met, and she looked away as if embarrassed at having been caught. Then Lupita turned back to look at me, as if to make sure I had seen her too, and I was still staring, and I wonder what my face must've looked like. I can only imagine. And all I could think was, *Why the hell is Ernie Rocha's girl staring at me?*

It continued like that for the rest of summer school. Locked eyes and smiles and me wondering what we were doing, what kind of game this was. What messages were being exchanged? Was she trying to tell me something? I just knew that I liked it. It was a thrill. Sometimes I thought that maybe others would see us, someone would catch me or catch her, but no one was paying attention. We could have been completely alone in that room.

One day, just a few classes before the end of summer school, my weight-lifting partner, Dave—a soccer player and one of the few white kids in the class—and I decided to use the decline bench, which is exactly what it sounds like: a bench angled downward. We hadn't used it before, so we had to hesitantly test the weights before starting. I went first, and just as I lifted the bar off the rack and brought it down to my chest, someone pushed Dave out of the way. In a panicked instant I glimpsed two shaved heads and laughing smiles surrounded by sparse black facial hair. A sour-smelling gym shirt was placed over my face. Two sets of hands grabbed my legs, and two more kept the bar pinned to my chest. I struggled to free myself, but the effort was futile. I could hear them laughing and telling me, "You're not supposed to use this bench! This is what happens to those who use this bench!" And I could hear Dave saying in a shrill voice, "We didn't know, we didn't." I kept crying out, probably just as shrilly, "Let go of me! Let go of me!"

Then the smelly shirt slipped off my face, allowing me to breathe clearly, but it also allowed me to see the girls returning from playing badminton. Of all days to be let out early! Who knows how long I was pinned like that. I never learned my assailants' objective, never learned why the decline bench was forbidden, and even to this day when I enter the gym and see someone use it I am hesitant, waiting for a group of vatos to jump out and restrain him. Finally I heard a girl's voice say, "Stop it, stop it, he's my friend," and I knew instantly whose voice it was, and what was before embarrassment and confusion now became mortified shame. Once the weight was lifted from me and the two guys set my legs free and I was able to rise from the bench, I couldn't bear to look up. I couldn't bear to look in her direction, not even to thank her. I just heard Dave asking, "Are you okay, dude? Why did they do that?"

Toward the end of class one of the kids who'd held my legs said, "We were just playing, homie." I nodded as if I knew that. Then the others came over and said the same thing, halfheartedly, as if someone had made them apologize. I tried to laugh it off, but my embarrassment hadn't lessened. I still couldn't seek out Lupita's eyes. Our eyes never met again that summer. I made sure of it. This is what she remembered later—not me pinned against the decline bench, red faced, struggling with all my might to free myself from my shameless aggressors; she just assumed that was boys roughhousing and forgot about it. What she remembered is how she kept looking for me, but I had stopped looking for her.

The next school year we didn't have any classes together, so we would only occasionally pass each other in the hall, and then always surrounded by friends, but still her eyes would find me and she'd smile, but no longer did I think, *Why is Ernie's girl smiling at me?* I was just sure she was being friendly.

Just before graduation, when everyone was signing yearbooks and passing out wallet-sized senior photos, giddy for the end of the year and whatever was to come next, I was seated on a bench, having just finished my lunch. I was alone reading a book—I can't remember which, but given the time in my life I want to say it was Camus's *The Stranger*—wishing to withdraw as much as possible from the excitement, for I felt little. I was heading to the East Coast—not to an Ivy League as I'd hoped, but to a respectable school nonetheless—and I wanted to be there already. I had disliked high school, I was tired of feeling hindered, unchallenged, and I was sure that college would be the exact opposite of the small-mindedness I thought infected everyone around me. Tony Galíndez called me a snob. I told him it was more complicated than that. "Fine," he'd say, "but do you always have to be reading a fucking book, like your isolation needs a prop?" Tony's honesty was brutal. But that semester he had a different lunch period, so I maintained my isolation and kept the book. Just as I was about to get up and toss my lunch bag in the garbage, I heard a girl say, "Aren't you going to give me a senior photo?"

Immediately I knew it was Lupita. I don't know how I knew her voice so well. I looked up and she was standing there, holding her yearbook on her hip. I got a whiff of her perfume, still vanilla and peaches after all these years. She was smiling, her jet-black hair pulled back so tight it almost made her eyes look askew, to an astonishing effect. I glanced behind her, I don't know why, maybe to see if anyone else was with her, but she was alone, and the closest kids were a group of freshmen twenty feet away throwing bottle caps at a crack in the concrete.

"I heard you're going to school in New York," she said.

"Close by. Connecticut," I said. "What are you going to be doing?"

She shrugged and said, "Nothing like that . . . We'll see what happens."

Then we were quiet for a moment and I didn't know what to say except to tell her I didn't have a senior portrait. I did, I just didn't want to pass it out. My mother had insisted I wear this shiny, periwinkle-blue dress shirt she'd bought me for my birthday, and in the photo it looks purple. To make things worse, I'm also surrounded by white daisies.

Lupita looked around self-consciously, or anxiously, and I thought I saw her jaw clench. Suddenly I wondered if we were being watched from a distance. I hadn't forgotten her brothers, or her brothers' friends, or Ernie's friends. Ernie had friends everywhere. Could this conversation be misinterpreted? I knew that very few guys dared talk to Lupita, definitely not without Ernie being present, but I figured I was safe enough. Who would suspect me of trying anything with Lupita Valdez? But I didn't care to test my immunity. I was about to stand up and invent some excuse to get away, when Lupita quickly stepped forward and handed me a small photo. She almost pressed it into my palm. Then she said good-bye, breathlessly, as if it pained her to say it, and before I could respond, even to say thank you or good-bye or to lamely blurt out, "Good luck" or "Have a good summer," she was gone. I watched her turn the corner before looking at the photo. I remember that the first thought that came to my mind was that the portrait wasn't flattering at all. I thought it strange that she wasn't photogenic. Her features looked somewhat unbalanced—her nose protruded, her smile was too big. I must've stared at the photo for a long time, because I was suddenly aware that I hadn't turned it over to see if something was written on the back. I did, and there in small, girly handwriting, full of loops and hearts dotting the i's, she had written, "I can tell you are someone special. I wish we had been able to get to know one another better. I pray to God that one day He might bring our paths together again. I want to wish you good luck. Remember me. Lupita."

I looked up and scanned the quad area as if someone were watching me and knew the words I'd just read. Across the way there was a group of cholos sitting on a concrete bench. Two of them were facing my direction, but dark shades masked their gaze. One of them was bouncing a blue handball. I could hear the repeated hollow pop as the rubber ball hit the pavement. Something made me feel deeply uneasy at that moment. I hadn't done anything wrong, I knew that, but I felt guilty of something. I put the photo in between a textbook and didn't look at it again until I got home. Then I placed it in a storage bin, underneath a stack of papers and mementos, and I didn't look at it again for four more years.

II

When I left for the East Coast I no longer wanted to think about high school or even Woodland for that matter. I never fit in, I had no close connections; it always felt as if it was just something I had to get through on the way to someplace else. I hated its blandness, the mind-numbing flatness of the agricultural valley. The terra-cotta-roofed tract-home developments, the strip malls, the chain stores, the fast-food restaurants and used-car dealerships. The historic downtown irked me too, as if a hundred years could be considered history. I even found myself tired of the incessant Mexican and white divide, as if there were only two kinds of people in the world, and I was forever stuck in between. I looked forward to a place where none of that mattered anymore. Where I could just be. Nestled in rolling wooded hills, my college's Gothic Revival architecture mixed with old colonial brick, picturesque green quads, and cobblestone paths couldn't have felt farther away. When people asked where I was from I'd lie and say, "Close to San Francisco." Sacramento is closer, but I guess even that was too provincial for me. Woodland became just a place I visited on vacations, and even then I hardly left the house. Tony Galíndez would ask me to come hang out, but I always found some excuse, and eventually he stopped trying.

So it took a strange set of circumstances for Lupita to enter the forefront of my thoughts again, but it was actually Ernie Rocha who entered my mind first. In my junior year, my friends Matt Helke and Chris Ralph, both tall gangly kids from New Hampshire, convinced me to join a fraternity. We were roommates together in Helms Hall. I wasn't a fraternity type, of course, and neither were my friends, but sophomore year they'd gone to a few rush events and had miraculously been tapped, and it seemed to have raised their social standing. At least they thought so, and maybe in the back of my mind, whenever they came back gaily rehashing the weekend's events, I envied them. There were a lot of jocks in the fraternity—hockey, lacrosse, and football players—but my roommates weren't, so I thought I'd be fine. I had heard the initiation process was grueling— drinking obscene amounts of alcohol, running ridiculous errands in the middle of the night, dressing up and dancing around Commons Dining Hall, fighting naked in the snow— but they assured me that they'd be my Big Brothers and would go easy on me. And they were. I had fun, even during the embarrassing stunts like having to dress up as a French maid during lunch and collect the fraternity brothers' trays once

15

they'd finished. Other guys had to do demeaning stuff too—walk around wearing a huge diaper or nothing but a sock on their dick—but those were worse, I thought. The only part that somewhat bothered me was the fact that everyone was instructed to call me Gonzalez. It's not my last name, of course, but one of the brothers thought it'd be funny, and so it stuck.

Well, on the final day of initiation we had a banquet and everyone dressed up in suits, and we reserved the back room at an exclusive eating club called the Sentry. It had wood-paneled walls cluttered with old photographs, red leather chairs, and elegant table settings, and it was best known for its drinking traditions and stuffy dress requirement. I wore a suit I'd bought just for the occasion. Dinner was served and we had plenty of punch, which must've been strong because it wasn't long before everyone was piss drunk. All the new initiates sat at the middle table, leaving us free game for the fraternity brothers. This was to be their last opportunity to treat us like shit before we all became equals. Over the years the fraternity had gained the reputation of being full of pricks and assholes, which they thought was unfounded, and somehow this developed into a tradition where on the last night the fraternity brothers would act like the pricks and assholes they were assumed to be. I was never quite sure of the logic there. All I knew was that everything was fair game. *Everything.* Two guys had to entertain the roomful with a song-and-dance routine about their mothers. One of their moms had died of breast cancer. Then the two guys who had walked around Commons naked except for socks on their dicks were asked to repeat the stunt, but this time they had to face each other and hold hands as they took turns listing off each other's girlfriends' attributes. Another guy named Sam Kensington and I were called into a side room and given outfits—me the French maid costume again, which I was allowed to wear over my suit, and Sam a cheap Halloween policeman outfit. They told us to run into the room and Sam was supposed to chase me around.

"If he catches you, Gonzalez," I was instructed, "you'll have to drink the entire bowlful of punch."

I got a head start, bursting into the room, everyone cheering. Sam the policeman came after me, and I ran around the tables, chairs and feet or entire legs placed in my way as obstacles. Everyone was laughing, including myself. Drunk as I was, all I could think was that there was no way in hell I was going to drink that bowl of punch—and they definitely would have made me drink it to the last drop.

It was a while before I heard what some of the brothers were chanting. "Catch the illegal, catch the illegal!" they cried. "Don't let another Mexican maid cross the border!" I laughed with them, realizing the gimmick: the policeman was supposed to be the border patrol chasing not a French maid but a Mexican one. I avoided the other guy with even greater purpose, as if once understanding why I needed to escape the policeman I acted the part. My shirt was drenched with sweat and I was getting dizzy. Finally, they called an end to the cat-and-mouse chase, and the other guy had to drink the sterling-silver bowlful of punch. I had won! I was relieved. I really didn't want to finish off all that alcohol. I started to take off the maid outfit when one of the brothers, a blond-haired kid with a neck that seemed to extend wider than his ears, rushed forward and said in a harsh voice, "Keep it on, Gonzalez! Get up and stand in the middle of your table!"

I looked at him, exasperated. "Come on," I said.

"Are you challenging me, Gonzalez?" he demanded.

"No, no," I said, and then I mumbled something about him being a little excessive. This seemed to piss him off and he repeated the order, this time loud enough that the room grew quiet. I realized I wasn't in a position to argue, so I stepped onto my chair then carefully found my footing amid the plates and drinking glasses. My legs felt weak from the exertion. I had a moment to look around the room, everyone staring up at me, flushed cheeks and drunken smiles.

"Mop the floor, Gonzalez," someone yelled out.

"What?" I asked, only because I was unsure where the voice had come from. Someone else called out, "Mop the floor, Gonzalez!"

This was met with laughter and a few cries of encouragement.

I pretended like I was mopping the table. Then one of the lead brothers yelled at me, "Faster!" I went a little faster. At some point a chant began, "Gonzalez! Gonzalez!" I then heard some pitiful attempts at gritos and shouts of "Arriba! Arriba!"

I found myself laughing even though by now I wanted my moment in the spotlight to be over. I looked at my fellow initiates and they were laughing too. Were they wondering why I was getting it worse than they were? Probably not. Because my Big Brothers were my close friends, everyone assumed I'd had an easier initiation. They must've thought I was finally getting my fair share. Another one of the brothers, a short, stocky wrestler, came over and pretended to rip away my make-believe mop.

"Now wash dishes!" he ordered. Veins were popping out of his forehead.

Reluctantly, I simulated washing a plate. My paltry resistance only seemed to fuel him on.

"You got a lot of dishes to get through!" he yelled.

"Is that so?" I said, still doing a half-assed job of dishwashing.

"Oh, so the lazy Mexican doesn't want to work, is that what I'm hearing?" he said, his eyes growing wide. "Now we gotta support you and your ten kids?"

"I don't have ten kids," I said.

I stood firm and waited for someone to come to my rescue. I looked for Matt and Chris in the crowd, but all I could see were dark suits and ties and white tablecloths.

Someone called out, "Just wash the dishes, Gonzalez! Don't be a lazy Mexican."

"You heard him!" the wrestler said. I looked down at him and could tell he wasn't joking anymore. His face was beet red and his eyes told me that what may have started playfully was now in his mind a simple matter of me listening to him. Some of the guys were like that: the momentary power over their initiates made them tyrannical, yet they expected it all to be forgiven once we were brothers.

It felt like I'd been standing on the table for ten minutes; maybe it was more, maybe less. I just knew I'd finally had enough. I moved to get off, but two bruisers with gigantic hands jumped out of nowhere to prevent me. It was never more apparent that I'd joined a fraternity of meatheads, all of them many times my size. I was helpless. The chant continued. Some clapped in unison. I couldn't believe it; was it really that funny of a joke? Did they need to see it to its conclusion? Again I looked around the room for Matt and Chris, but everyone was a blur. My need for it to be over was approaching desperation. Still, I found myself smiling. I couldn't help it. I felt the strange sensation that if I stopped smiling I'd burst into tears, and I knew that couldn't happen.

So maybe everyone thought I was okay with the prank, and maybe I would've been if it had ended there. Right there at that precise moment. If I'd been allowed to step off the table and take my place with the other initiates. But they kept me up there, and soon I found a face that wasn't chanting. His dark face was like stone, and I noticed him because a brown face—let alone a face like stone—stood out among all those drunken, gleeful smiles. His name was Albert, a big Chicano kid from Arizona. He had a thick goatee and a nose that looked as if it had been broken several times. He'd been a lineman on the football team, but he tore his ACL in his junior year and quickly got fat and out of shape.

I stared at him and he stared back, and for a second I thought maybe I was looking at him for help, but I saw in his eyes that he didn't feel sympathy for me. In fact, there was hatred in his expression, as if the entire insult was against him and I'd allowed it. As if I was just a white kid with a Spanish surname playing the part of a Mexican maid for the pleasure of a roomful of jackasses. Well, weren't those jackasses his friends too? Didn't he see this was painful for me as well? Of course not; I was grinning like an idiot.

The chanting continued, the room more and more a blur. And then for reasons I can't exactly explain—maybe because Albert resembled him—Ernie Rocha flashed through my mind. All in an instant, I pictured him strolling into class, his clothes perfectly pressed, his denim Dickies work jacket making him appear larger than he was. I pictured him confident and assured, afraid of nothing. Maybe I thought of him at that moment because I knew that Ernie Rocha would've never found himself in a situation like this. Humiliated. It was just a prank made in poor taste, I kept telling myself. That was the point, and everyone got his share, not just me. So why humiliation, why not just plain embarrassment? I don't know. All I know is that I finally stopped smiling, and once I did, I burst into tears.

Most of the room quieted, but not everyone. I heard a voice say, "Is Gonzalez fucking crying?" And then again, "Is Gonzalez fucking crying?" Some continued their chant with even greater enthusiasm, as if this was the result they were looking for. My two roommates finally stepped forward from a back corner table and pushed the instigator out of the way. I climbed off the table, the need to sob growing stronger. I walked out of the room, staring at the ground. Through tears I looked up briefly and saw faces, confused and concerned, as if they didn't know what part in my breakdown they had just played. I made it out of the room and into a green-carpeted hallway, and there I began to sob uncontrollably, and I continued even when Matt and Chris found me and kept asking, "What happened, man? What's wrong?"

"I don't know, I don't know," I kept repeating.

"They were just joking with you," Matt said. "It was just a joke. We all had to go through it."

"We thought you were laughing," Chris said.

"I know, I know, just let me be," I said.

I left the restaurant alone. It was freezing cold. After a few stares, I realized I was still wearing the French maid outfit on top of my suit. I stepped into a dark entryway, climbed out of the outfit, and then stuffed it in a garbage can. Needless to say, I didn't join the fraternity.

A few weeks later, drunk and alone in my room, I sat looking out the window at the snow falling on the cobblestone courtyard. Feeling sorry for myself, and wanting some form of company, I decided to call Tony Galíndez.

"Tony," I said when he picked up. "It's me."

He laughed and said, "Of course I know it's you, fool, you think your voice has changed or what?"

We talked for almost forty-five minutes, and at one point he asked if I was drunk. I told him a little, and then I asked him why. He told me that he hadn't remembered me sounding so happy in a long time. "Happy?" I asked, feeling quite the opposite. "I guess it's just nice to talk to you," I said.

He called me a homo.

Toward the end of the conversation, running out of things to say, my drunkenness wearing off, I asked him if he knew what Ernie Rocha was up to. He was silent on the other end before saying, "You didn't hear?"

"No, what happened?"

"They killed him," he said.

"What? Ernie?"

"Yeah, they found his body by his car with two bullets in the back of his head. Over there at the Triple Nickel on Matmor. The police said it was a failed robbery, but everyone knows that he'd been mixed up in some bad shit before it happened. They said he'd gotten into selling drugs, but you know how Ernie was, he was discreet. If he was involved he never slipped up. People just talk a lot of shit."

Our conversation didn't last much longer. I hung up the phone, wishing I hadn't called, wishing I didn't know that Ernie was dead. My memories of him resurfaced. I found a flask of cheap whiskey in the common room and drank some more. I thought about Ernie for a long time, and then, at some point, I thought of Lupita Valdez, and I felt so sorry for her that I began to cry. At least that's why I thought I was crying. I was also drunk, the long winters depressed me, I missed home, and Ernie Rocha was the first person in my life to die.

CHAPTER TWO

I

I SAW HER on a Tuesday at the Yolo County Mall in Woodland. I needed new shoes. I was in my second year of a doctoral program in history at UC Davis. I applied to a lot of different schools, almost all of them on the East Coast. I applied to Davis as a backup, just in case, I told myself. Turns out it was the only place I got in. At first I was disappointed, but deep down I realized it's where I wanted to be. I felt adrift my entire four years at college. I didn't know why I was out there. I kept waiting for some reason to present itself, something that told me, definitively, *this* is why you're here. Before, I thought the East Coast held all the answers, but I had found none. I studied history because it interested me, but I felt no vocation for it. My advisor encouraged me to apply to graduate school, so I did. He spoke directly to his colleagues at other top programs. I thought I would have my choice, but in the end my only option was home. My parents were thrilled.

My classes and meetings were on Mondays, Wednesdays, and Fridays, which left Tuesdays and Thursdays free. The soles of my shoes had split open, which at first I didn't mind because I liked living the part of the poor student, but then it rained and my socks were soaked the minute I walked outside. So I drove the ten-mile stretch of highway to Woodland. The Yolo County Mall was empty as it always was, especially on a midweek morning. I walked into a few shoe stores but found nothing to my liking. There were stretches of the mall where I was completely alone except for a few cart vendors waiting in vain for customers. When I passed they didn't even look my way, as if they'd long given up hope. Most of the large chain stores had left years before. Only Mervyn's and Gottschalks remained. There were plenty of variety stores, shelves piled high with an

23

assortment of merchandise—blankets, sporting goods, toys, and cheap jewelry. The turnover rate was so high that it was hard to believe any business took the chance.

I found a pair of brown leather loafers I liked at Mervyn's. I sat down to try them on and I felt someone's presence nearby. I looked up and found a pair of dark eyes staring directly at me. I quickly turned away and pretended to examine the tag on the shoebox. From my brief glance I could tell the girl was beautiful. I wondered why she was looking at me. I lifted my head slightly, and out of the top corner of my eye I could see that she was still on the other side of a dress-shoe display. She was just standing there with her hands at her side, making no pretense of occupying herself. Then I realized it was probably a sales associate wanting to make sure I didn't need assistance. I hesitantly looked in her direction again.

"I thought that was you," she said.

Her hair was pulled back tight in a bun, just as it was the day she gave me her photo, the last time I saw her. She looked the same as I remembered. Almond-shaped eyes surrounded by long eyelashes. Her nose was thin, almost beak-like. Her skin was golden brown, smooth and unblemished. She didn't wear as much makeup as she did in high school, nor were her eyebrows plucked as thin, and she'd ditched the large hoop earrings for smaller ones. She was wearing a dark-gray suit with a name tag on her lapel. I don't know why, but I stared at the name tag.

"Lupita," she said.

"I know," I said. "I remember you."

Her face flushed and her smile grew so wide that her long, thick eyelashes obscured her eyes. We were both quiet for a moment. I thought to ask her how she'd been, what she'd been up to, but I could see that she was nervous or caught off guard, and this confused me. What did she have to be nervous about? Our silence continued and she kept looking at me, a dazed smile on her face. Several times she reached for her earring, then her brass bracelet, then back to her earring. I just smiled dumbly.

"So you're buying shoes?" she finally asked, pointing at the open box I held in my hand. I realized I had one shoe off. I looked down at my pathetic-looking damp sock. I started explaining that my old shoes had split at the sole and my socks were constantly getting wet with the recent rainy weather and that it was distracting to sit through class with wet socks, until finally I stopped myself and asked, "Do you work here?" I pointed to her name tag.

"I'm a sales manager," she said. "I work here and at a few other Mervyn's in the area. Hey, I'm actually about to take a break. Do you want to get coffee?"

It took me a second to realize she was asking me to accompany her. My hesitation must have discouraged her, because she followed with, "Or maybe another time."

"No, no," I told her, "let's go."

"Okay, I'll be right back. I need to lock up my office."

Not thinking clearly, I put my old shoe back on, covered the box I held in my hands, and brought it to the register. I wasn't even sure the shoes fit. I hadn't looked at the price either. They were expensive. "They're that much?" I asked the sales associate.

"Yes. Do you still want them?"

It felt easier to say yes. I paid, and then, bag in hand, waited in the shoe section for Lupita to return. This time I saw her from across the store, heading toward me. She was staring in my direction. I stared in hers and she looked away, glancing to her right, and then at her watch. I looked away too, glancing down at the shiny linoleum floor, and then at my receipt, which I still held in my hand. I noted once again the expense, and then I turned back to look at her. I couldn't believe how beautiful she was. She was closer now and staring at me again, and I thought it so strange that I'd woken up this morning thinking of nothing except that I had to buy new shoes.

"Are you ready?" she asked.

"Yes," I said.

We walked out of Mervyn's and into the empty mall, so empty that I could hear the echo of her high heels. She told me that she usually only had fifteen minutes, but today her supervisor was gone so she could take as long as she wanted. I asked her about her job and she started telling me how she began working at Mervyn's right after high school and had been promoted quickly. "It's all right," she said. "It pays the bills, but I still live at home. My parents won't let me leave, or I should say my parents *and* my brothers."

Without really thinking, I asked how they were.

"Who, my brothers?" she asked, surprised. "Do you really want to know?"

I shrugged my shoulders. "I guess I was just asking," I said.

She laughed and then sighed. "Oh, you know, they'll always be the same, right?"

"Yeah, true," I said, chuckling in acknowledgement even though I could only assume what she was talking about.

We didn't end up getting coffee. I thought we were heading to some place on the other side of the mall, but once we reached the end of the mall, where the entrance to a now-defunct department store was shuttered, we turned and headed back. I don't remember all that was said; we mostly just caught up on the years since high school, though I asked most of the questions and she did most of the talking. I didn't ask her about Ernie. I figured if she wanted to talk about him, she would. A half hour passed before she checked her watch and said she had to get back.

"Weren't we going to get coffee?" I asked.

She laughed, "Oh, yeah, I forgot! What was I thinking? We can still get some if you'd like."

"It's okay," I said.

"You sure?"

"Yeah, I'll walk you back though."

We returned to Mervyn's, neither of us saying much. I couldn't think of any more questions to ask her. As we approached the entrance, she turned to me and touched my arm briefly before letting her hand drop. She was biting her bottom lip and her eyes were wide. "Can I tell you something embarrassing?" she said.

"Of course," I said, though honestly I couldn't fathom what

embarrassing thing she had to tell me. I waited for some innocuous anecdote about a broken umbrella or slipping on a wet floor or something a coworker had told her. But without hesitating or any sign of self-consciousness, she told me that in high school she'd had the biggest crush on me. For two years every time she saw me she would become nervous and her mind would go blank. All she could do was smile.

Before her confession I hadn't felt any need to be nervous, even though I kept thinking to myself, *I can't believe I'm walking around the mall with Lupita Valdez.* In fact, I was strangely cool considering I was in the presence of a girl I worshipped in high school. But suddenly I was nervous. It was a good nervous though. I was flattered. I found myself chuckling like an idiot, saying, "Really? Really?" I didn't mind this piece of news at all. It made my high school years seem less pathetic. "I wondered why our eyes always met," I said. "I thought it was just coincidence, or that I was going crazy."

"No, no, you weren't going crazy," she said. Then she informed me that she had never told anyone this before, not one person, not even Carla, her best friend, because she didn't think anyone would understand.

"Understand?" I asked.

"Well, you know, why I liked you." Before I could be offended, she added, "We weren't exactly in the same crowd."

"That's true," I said.

"So you're the first person I've told."

Then she waited, looking at me expectantly, as if it was now my turn to respond or make a similarly revealing confession. But I didn't know what to say, so I said the first thing that came to mind. "But weren't you dating Ernie?"

I regretted it as soon as I said it. His name fell like a brick on our playful reminiscing, as if what we were talking about was so long ago that it no longer mattered, but it did. Now it did, at least, and I saw her face darken, and she said, "I was with Ernie, but I was young, plus it was just a crush," and she said it in a way that I knew I'd offended her, as if I was judging her somehow.

"I'm sorry," I said.

"Why?" she asked. "There's no need."

And then we were quiet for a moment and she said she should get going. "It was good seeing you," I said, and she said the same thing, and then we were walking away from one another, and I could hear her heels echoing in the empty mall, and I wanted to turn back and say, "We should get together again sometime." But I didn't.

That night I went to bed thinking of Lupita Valdez's crush on me. I imagined turning back the clock. I pictured the two of us together, holding hands after school, Lupita with her bright-red lipstick and wide smile, her hair pulled back, her large silver hoop earrings . . . and then me. But somehow I didn't fit into the picture. In my place, I kept imagining Ernie Rocha. He fit so much better. People would've just talked shit about me—*Why she with that nerdy white boy? Who the fuck is he? Who does he think he is? Her brothers actually let* him *date her?*—and of course, once I thought of her brothers I couldn't help but remember that in order to date Lupita you had to fight them. I actually tried to imagine it. I saw myself waiting for them in the school parking lot, dressed up as a cholo, wearing a hairnet and tank top with my last name tattooed in Old English on my back, and people whispering, "I didn't know that fool was Mexican." What they also didn't know is that instead of spending all my time studying I'd actually been training with a tae kwon do grandmaster . . . And then I must have fallen asleep because I don't remember anything after that.

Two days later, Thursday, I went to return the shoes. They didn't really fit and I'd paid too much and the only reason why I wouldn't have returned them was because I'd be afraid of running into Lupita again. When I asked myself why I'd be afraid of running into her, I had no good reason except that pursuing beautiful girls—actually any girl—made me anxious. But I wasn't pursuing her, I decided. So I went. I returned the shoes, looking around the entire time, thinking I'd see her. I lingered for a while in the men's section. I browsed for shirts I didn't really need and couldn't afford. Finally, I left the store, disappointed. I realized that I did in fact want to see Lupita, and that returning the shoes was just an excuse to see her again. So I walked back inside and headed toward her office. I passed a woman wearing a name tag and I asked if Lupita was working that day.

"Yes, but she's on break," she said. "Can I help you?"

I mumbled something about being a friend and left the department store. I took a chance and walked toward the only coffee shop in the mall, which we'd passed on Tuesday. I walked quickly, not wanting to miss her, though I guess we would've crossed paths if she was returning to work. I saw her through a window draped with an elaborately beaded curtain. The dimly lit café had an Indian décor; on the walls were framed photographs of the Taj Mahal and some other structures I didn't recognize. The place was nice, too nice for that mall (in fact, it wouldn't be there much longer). From where I approached she couldn't see me, but I could see her. She was alone. She held her coffee cup in both hands as if feeling its warmth, and she stared off into space as if pondering something that troubled her.

It was at this moment that I began to see her differently, beyond her beauty, beyond the Lupita Valdez I knew only from a distance in junior high and high school. I don't know what it was exactly, except that if she had been with friends or a coworker, or reading a magazine, or checking her cell phone, everything would have been different. It would've been just another chance passing. Maybe we would've shared another short, awkward conversation to fill the silence. But for that moment I watched her, lost in thought, and I knew that wherever she was in her head no one else had entered. Not even Ernie Rocha. There was something so sad about her sitting alone in this coffee shop, and I pictured her there every day, the same routine, sitting alone, holding the coffee between her hands, contemplating her life in silence, thoughts beyond me that I wished to understand.

I approached her quietly, said her name, and she looked up. She seemed happy to see me, but not surprised.

We started seeing more of one another. We'd meet for lunch mostly, but every now and then she'd call and ask if I wanted to grab dinner. We never went on what could definitively be called a date. It was always spontaneous, and then only for short periods of time, a couple of hours at most. Always she had to get home. Dinner was never followed by anything else, and for a while I didn't think much about it, but then slowly my neurotic tendencies kicked in and I began to wonder if the reason she had to get home was because she didn't want her brothers thinking she was out with someone. Honestly, I couldn't fathom that her brothers still maintained the rule of having to fight them in order to date her. We weren't in high school anymore. We were all adults now, and Lupita could take care of herself. Plus, it was a nonissue because I didn't think we were actually dating. We enjoyed one another's company, I knew that, but except for that first day when she talked about the crush she had on me in high school, we never talked about our feelings or about relationships or about the two of us in any sort of an intimate sense. I avoided any discussion about relationships, mainly because I didn't want to talk about Ernie, and she didn't ask me about my prior relationships, though if she had I wouldn't have had much to tell her—just a rather short list of casual hookups.

We never saw each other in Woodland. She always drove out to Davis, which was more convenient for me. There was also more to do; downtown Davis was close to the university, and there were restaurants, bars, bookstores, art galleries, coffee shops, ice-cream parlors, and movie theaters. The streets were perfect for taking a leisurely stroll, which was just about the opposite of Woodland, where it seemed a big diesel truck was always waiting impatiently for you to cross the street. So it made sense that we met in Davis and I never really questioned it, but one day I was in Woodland visiting my parents and I sent Lupita a text and asked if she wanted to get together.

"Sure!" she responded.

"I'm in Woodland," I wrote. "We can meet up here."

A half hour went by. I started to wonder what had happened. Finally she texted, "I got held up. Sorry :(How about we do tomorrow?"

"Okay," I wrote back, only a little disappointed.

But then she wrote, "And I can drive to you in Davis, K?"

Maybe I read into it too much, but that was the last time I suggested we meet in Woodland.

II

Lupita and I were finally able to spend more than a few hours together when she had a three-day training conference in Walnut Creek. One of her coworkers was staying with her in the hotel, but the woman had to leave after the second night, so Lupita had the last night alone. She called me and told me that she was thinking about skipping the afternoon session and maybe I could drive out and we could go to San Francisco or something. I had class that afternoon, but I didn't think twice about missing it. I drove the hour there, wondering the entire time whether or not I would be spending the night with her. A part of me still felt as if we were just friends hanging out. We hadn't moved beyond that, at least. There were awkward moments when we were saying good-bye, when I wondered whether I should kiss her, but I never did. It seemed like such an unnatural leap. We would always hug good-bye, and sometimes the embrace would last longer, and I would wonder if it was actually longer or if it was all in my head. Was it me who held on, or was it her?

I picked Lupita up at the hotel and we drove to the city. Her hair was down and she had changed out of the austere business attire that she wore whenever we were together because she never went home to change before seeing me. Now she had on a denim jacket over a white cotton dress with a canary-yellow belt. She wore yellow sandals too. She looked younger and smaller, and she seemed more excited than usual. She was talkative, chatty almost. She filled me in on how boring and pointless the training was; she described her coworkers, those she was close to and those she kept her distance from. I let her talk, asking questions from time to time, but I was happy to just listen, to hear her voice. We drove slowly through rush-hour traffic, passing through Berkeley and Oakland. As we approached the Bay Bridge, I couldn't stop thinking, *Who would have ever thought I'd be driving to San Francisco with Lupita Valdez?* At some point, waiting in the long line to pay the bridge toll, she placed her hand on top of mine. She didn't stop talking—it was as if she did it unthinkingly—and I turned my hand around to hold hers. My heart started to beat faster, and I worried that my palm was going to turn into a clammy mess. Then the car in front of us moved forward, and I had to put the car in gear, and I almost didn't want to because it meant letting go of her hand. But finally she laughed and said, "Go!"

After we crossed the Bay Bridge she asked me if I knew where I was going. I told her I had no idea, so we looked for exits, deciding to head to North Beach or the Pier, both places we'd been before, but long ago. I don't know where we ended up; we just decided to park finally, thinking we were close enough to something. We weren't. We walked around looking for a main avenue, but we must have turned on all the wrong ones. The closest was Market Street, and by that time we were so tired from walking that we decided to just grab bottled waters in a deli market. We sat on stools at a counter and looked out the window. She was beaming.

"What's up?" I asked.

"What do you mean?"

"Why are you smiling?"

She laughed. "I didn't know I was. I don't know, probably just excited to be here. I don't leave Woodland much."

Now I felt bad that we were sitting in a deli market. I should've planned something, looked up directions before-hand. I told her so, but she didn't seem to understand.

"I don't care," she said. "This is fun," and she turned back to looking out the window with that same smile on her face.

I remembered when we were in high school; the few times I would go with friends to visit San Francisco it'd be as if we were heading on an adventure. We never did much. We walked around for hours and ate slices of pizza because we were afraid to try anything else. Once we drove all the way to Ocean Beach and spent the afternoon freezing, but it didn't matter because it was the beach. Then we'd drive the hour and a half back to Woodland feeling as if we'd been gone for years and traveled halfway around the world. I had forgotten that. The expression on Lupita's face made me wonder if it was still the same for her.

We found North Beach finally, the streets packed with people, and we passed one restaurant and café after another. We ate at a restaurant with outdoor seating. Lupita picked the place for the waiters, all old Italian men in white jackets and bow ties. We sat outside, close to a heater because she was cold but she still wanted to be outside so she could see everything. I looked at the menu and saw the prices and knew the bill was going to make a dent in my monthly stipend. She must have sensed my thoughts because she told me right away, "This is on me. I invited you out here."

"No, it's all right," I said. "I can pay."

"But you're a student," she said. "I have a job."

"That doesn't matter, I'm supposed to pay," I said, only half joking.

"Oh, because you're the man?" she asked, her eyebrows raised teasingly.

"Yes," I said. "Exactly."

She laughed, and I wasn't sure what she found so funny: that I considered myself a man, or that I felt a need to adhere to traditional roles? For a moment, I thought about all the guys who had tried to date her over the years. I imagined they probably would've worked just so they could buy her expensive gifts and take her out on the weekends. They probably wouldn't have so much as let her open a door. But Lupita had a job, and she lived at home, and it was true, I was a student on a tight budget. So I let her pay without much resistance, and she seemed happy to take the check. I continued to think about it though. It bothered me, and when I paid for the gelato afterward I just felt more pathetic.

After the gelato, we walked around, and though we walked practically shoulder to shoulder we didn't hold hands. I asked if I could treat her to a glass of wine. She told me she didn't drink alcohol.

"Ever?" I asked.

"A few times," she said. "But I don't like it. We can go somewhere anyway. I'll have a soda or something."

We found some French place with 1920s art deco décor and we sat at the bar. I looked at the wine list and had no idea what I was looking at, so I just ordered the least expensive glass. Lupita asked for a Sprite. She was quiet and the smile that had been on her face all evening was gone. I wondered if something was wrong.

"So how come you don't like to drink?" I asked.

She looked down at her glass and mumbled, "I don't drink because I believe alcohol is unholy."

I thought for second she was joking and I smiled unsurely. "This is just fermented grapes," I said, sliding my wine glass toward her. "It's all just a natural process, fermentation, distillation, they've done it for thousands of years. Jesus and his disciples drank wine at their table, what could be unholy about it?"

Her eyes were downcast and she didn't respond right away. I wanted to change the subject. I wished we hadn't come to a bar. She was upset, and I couldn't understand why. Later I would understand better, when she told me about her alcoholic father, her alcoholic grandfather, her alcoholic uncles, and her soon-to-be alcoholic brothers—her life of dealing with men who slept eight hours, worked eight hours, and spent the remaining eight going through twelve packs of beer. But that night all she told me was, "It makes people do horrible things."

I should've just nodded my head, but I felt the need to say, "Well, everything in moderation, right?"

We drove back to Walnut Creek in silence, and finally, a little upset, I told her, "Look, I'm sorry that we don't agree on whether wine is holy or unholy, but all I had was one glass, and

I personally don't do horrible things when I drink, so can we please just let it go?"

Now it was my turn to witness her unsure smile.

"You're still thinking about that?" she asked.

"You're not?"

She laughed and told me that she wasn't thinking about that at all. She had stopped thinking about it as soon as the conversation had ended. I asked her why she was so quiet then, and she said, "I was thinking of whether or not to invite you to stay the night."

I sat back in the seat, digesting this piece of information. Now I felt stupid. I was sure the night was ruined. I had been picturing a long drive back to Woodland. "Well, what have you decided?" I asked.

"I don't know," she said, laughing gently, and she turned up the radio.

When we arrived at the hotel, I parked and she turned to me and said, "You should stay." But the way she said it, very matter-of-factly, made me think that maybe she just wanted to save me the late-night drive. It was much colder on this side of the bay and we hurried, Lupita clutching my arm, from the car to the hotel. Her room was on the second floor and down a long hall. When we entered I saw that there were two beds. She lay down on one, kicked off her yellow sandals, and stretched. "My God, I'm so tired," she said. "It's been a long day." I just stood there, unsure what to do next. I pretended to look at a generic painting on the wall, a still life of flowers. She rose from the bed, rummaged in her suitcase, and pulled out a toothbrush.

"Here's an extra one," she said. "I have sweats if you want to wear them. Do you need an undershirt?"

Then she disappeared into the bathroom, and I sat down on the edge of the bed, wondering if it was up to me to make a move. Of course it was, but then again, she seemed so anxious to get ready for bed. I found the remote and turned on the television. She emerged a few minutes later, her hair pulled back behind her head. She wore a white V-neck T-shirt and thin pajama bottoms. I did a double take. She looked even more striking now. This felt like a form of intimacy in itself, seeing her right before falling asleep. If that was all that happened that night I would've been satisfied. "The bathroom is yours," she said. I handed her the remote. She took it from me and immediately started flipping through channels. I brushed my teeth, washed my face, changed into the sweat pants, which fit me big, and walked out into the room. She had turned off the television and was under the covers, her head propped up by two pillows. Her eyes watched me. I headed toward the other bed and pulled back the covers.

She started to giggle. "What are you doing, silly?" she asked.

"We're going to bed, right?"

She laughed again. "Not over there," she said. "Sleep here," and she patted the bed as if instructing a child. I felt like one. She smiled as if she enjoyed my uncertainty. Why was I so unsure of the situation? After a halfway attempt to put the covers back in place, and then realizing I didn't need to, I left them and grabbed one of the pillows. I crawled in next to her.

"Are you okay?" she asked, as she scooted closer to me, still with the same smile on her face. I turned toward her. Now I pulled her close, more forcefully than I intended, as if my instincts had tired of my doubts and inaction. Our bodies touched and I realized there was no repeating this moment, ever, our two bodies touching for the first time, fitting together like they were meant to be together (even through sweat pants and pajama bottoms). I held her tightly, feeling it hard to breathe, as if I had forgotten how. I drew her face toward mine and looked into her eyes. I leaned in to kiss her, and at that moment I thought to myself, *I am kissing Lupita Valdez, I am kissing Ernie's girl.* I tried to remove the thought from my mind, but I couldn't. *I am kissing Lupita Valdez, I am kissing Ernie's girl. Damn it*, I thought, *why am I thinking of him now?* And then I realized that her cheeks were wet, and I opened my eyes and saw that she was crying. I pulled away, but she pulled my head closer and continued kissing me. I could feel her wet cheeks against mine. Why was she crying? Was she thinking of Ernie too, crying because he was dead, because she still loved

36

him? Was he the last person she was with? She pulled away finally, maybe sensing that I was no longer there either. And she placed her head on my chest, and I held her tightly, and I wanted to ask her why she was crying, but I didn't say anything. We were just quiet.

After a few minutes, she sighed and said, "We're going to have to take this slow."

III

When Lupita and I were out I was always conscious of the stares men gave her. She walked into a room and turned heads. It was as if I wasn't there. As if we were walking together by chance. Men eyed her hungrily, they eyed her in awe, already lovestruck. They eyed her without knowing I was staring right back at them. It was hard not to be bothered by this. I think Lupita had ignored men's stares for so long that she didn't even think about it. She probably didn't realize I felt like her luggage or her little brother or at most (and at worst) her boyfriend who was too insignificant to give a damn about.

One evening we decided to go eat in midtown Sacramento. It was dark by the time we finished. On our way back to the car, which we had parked on a side street, we passed a group of young guys in straight-brimmed baseball hats sitting on the stoop of a dilapidated Victorian. They were drinking 40s from paper bags. As we approached, their conversation quieted and so did ours. I can't remember what it was I was telling her, just that I was the one talking. Instinctively our pace quickened and Lupita grabbed my arm tighter. I had a feeling they were going to say something, and inside I was saying, *Please don't say anything, please just let us pass by without saying anything.* I expected something minor, a whistle or some passing comment, but one of the guys actually stood up and blocked our way.

We stopped abruptly, momentarily unsure where to go, but then he stepped aside and gestured that he was allowing us to continue walking. When we passed him, he kept close to Lupita, pelvis thrust forward, as if following her with his eyes was not enough, his entire body had to follow along as well. His facial features were lost in the shadow of his hat and hooded sweat shirt, but then he lifted his face just enough for me to see his mocking smile. "Damn, girl, looking good," he said in a high-pitched whine. "Why don't you kick it here with me and my boys?" He cackled, and then just as quickly as he appeared, he skipped back to rejoin his friends.

I breathed a sigh of relief and Lupita's grip around my arm relaxed.

One of the guys on the stoop called after us, "How you gonna let him talk to your girlfriend like that?"

"What a little bitch!" another followed.

For the briefest second I thought of stopping and turning around. My heart was racing as I imagined the confrontation, but by then we had already turned a corner and it was too late to say or do anything. We were silent until Lupita said, "What was that you were saying before?"

I tried to continue the conversation, but as I spoke all I could think about was the guy insulting her, insulting me, and the fact that I had done nothing. I did absolutely nothing! Suddenly I was awash in ideas of what I should have done. I should have said, "Have some respect," or, "*Show* some respect." I don't know why the distinction in words made a difference, but it seemed important at the time. I even imagined what would've happened if I had punched the guy or tripped him. He was drunk. Maybe I could have taken him. I even thought of telling Lupita to go on ahead without me and going back to confront them. That way at least she wouldn't have to see what transpired, whatever it was—my inglorious beating probably—but she'd at least know I'd done something. Then I caught myself. I was making myself sick to my stomach.

On our way back to Davis we were silent. I couldn't stop thinking about the incident, especially the taunt directed at me. She must have sensed it because when we were about half-way home she said, "There's nothing you could have done."

"I know," I said.

We were silent again.

"Then why is it still bothering you?" she asked.

"Because he insulted you," I said, "and I didn't do anything, and then I got called out on it."

"But they were just being asses," she said. "They wanted to provoke you. You think it mattered to me what he said? You think it offended me? Of course not. So why should it offend you?"

I was silent, thinking about this. She was right. So then why couldn't I let it go? Almost under my breath I muttered, "I feel like others would have done something, regardless."

"What?" she asked.

I repeated myself.

She knit her brow and looked at me as if she couldn't believe what she'd just heard. "Because they're idiots," she said.

"Ernie wouldn't have allowed it," I said.

"Ernie?" she scoffed. "Ernie? Are you serious? Well, Ernie's dead. You remember that?"

I didn't respond. I couldn't believe I'd actually brought up his name. But once it was out I didn't regret it. Ernie inspired fear, respect. Me? I didn't even exist. Any guy who so desired could say anything he liked, ogle her to his heart's content, and all I could do was watch or pretend I didn't notice. Was that really what she wanted?

We were quiet for another couple of minutes. Then Lupita said quietly, the disappointment evident in the coldness of her voice, "You know, I was first attracted to you because you were different. You weren't like the other guys I knew, like the guys who always tried to date me. You weren't like my brothers. You weren't like Ernie. You were just different. But little did I know you suffer from the same pride."

"It's not pride," I said.

"Well, then what is it?"

"I don't know . . . insecurity."

"Same thing," she said, turning to face me. Her voice rose and started to crack. "Ernie and I broke up before he was killed because I couldn't stand the rules he lived by. The same rules as my brothers. He thought he needed to provide for me, be my protector, my savior—well, I never asked for that. And I never asked you. So don't. Just don't."

"Okay," I said. Then, after a long silence, I asked, "So—you and Ernie had already broken up?"

"Yeah," she said. Then she fell back in her seat and faced the road, silent the entire way back to Davis. I kept trying to get a side-glance at her profile to gauge how upset she was, but it was too dark. I had no idea what she was thinking. When we arrived at her car, I thought we would talk some more. I wanted to apologize for overthinking the situation, but when I shut off the engine, she quickly opened her door, mumbled something about calling me, and got out and shut the door behind her. I watched her walk away and thought I saw her wipe her eyes. I contemplated calling after her, but I settled for a long, defeated sigh.

I really hated those guys on the stoop at that moment. I wanted to drive back to Sacramento and crash my car into their little gathering. Instead, I sat parked for a good ten minutes imagining what I could've done or said to save face in that situation. Pride, honor, insecurity, maybe they were the same thing, but how could she expect me not to be affected? I replayed the confrontation over in my mind. A physical response was, of course, out of the question—I knew I'd never be quick enough on my feet. So I thought of a few comebacks, each one lamer than the last. Finally, I came up with this: the next time some idiot made a comment to me about Lupita, I would simply say, "*There* you go, buddy." That's it, and just walk on. It was casual indifference, neither provocation nor retreat. I thought it brilliant. So much so that when I returned to my room that night I found myself repeating it over and over. *There you go, buddy. Yeah, you think you're funny, you think you're tough, you think you can talk about my girl like that . . .* Soon I was shirtless and shadowboxing in the mirror. It wasn't long before I was out of breath. I collapsed on my bed, hugging a pillow, wishing it were Lupita. I wondered what exactly had made her cry. I fell asleep worried that she was going to break up with me.

We saw less of each other over the next couple of weeks. I was certain her feelings for me had waned, if not disappeared completely. There was no ostensible change in the way she behaved toward me, at least not at first, but as more days passed between visits my doubts grew. When we did finally get together I was on edge; I felt a distance, and I assumed that distance came from her. After our first kiss that night in her hotel room our physical intimacy was infrequent. We held hands in the car, sometimes. She hugged me good-bye and lingered, sometimes. We kissed only once or twice more, and on my own initiative, which she responded to but which she also ended, pulling away and looking around herself nervously, making me feel as if I had done something I shouldn't have. To my mind, once intimacy began it should only grow, but we seemed to have regressed and remained there. I understood she wanted to take things slow, but maybe she also wanted to keep me at arm's length; maybe now that her high school crush had been realized, she didn't want more. I even convinced myself that I was tiring of the periodic meetings—a lunch here, a brief dinner there. We were just two friends from high school hanging out, and what was the point of that? I needed to know where this was going. I decided that I would say something the next time we met up.

It was a Tuesday during her lunch break and she met me in Davis. She was distracted; issues at work were bogging her down, her manager was putting pressure on her, she had to go to the Sacramento store that afternoon to inquire about purchasing or inventory or for some reason that I only half listened to. I kept thinking about how to segue into a conversation about our relationship, but I quickly gave up. It wasn't the right time. Plus, maybe I was tiring of the periodic meetings, but that didn't mean I wanted them to end. After lunch I walked her back to her car and she asked me if I was okay.

"Everything's fine," I told her. "Why do you ask?" For a moment I wondered if she was going to initiate the conversation herself, inform me that after giving it some thought she did, in fact, want a boyfriend who could beat up potential harassers. But she merely said, "You seem distracted."

Again I told her everything was fine.

"When can we see each other again?" she asked, and she said it with a hint of desperation, so slight I thought I was mistaken.

"Whenever," I said.

"Whenever?" she said. "What does that mean?"

"It means when you have time. You're the one who always determines when we see each other."

"Well, you know you can ask me too," she said, her eyes looking directly into mine. She looked hurt. "It seems like it's always up to me."

Now I knew for sure that there was desperation in her voice. I was confused. Why would she be desperate to see me when all she needed to do was ask?

"How about tonight, then?" I said, surprising myself. "Come to my place and we'll make dinner."

I was sure she was going to tell me that she couldn't, that she had to be home early or that she had other plans, but she agreed.

So I rushed home, cleaned up my studio, bought food to fill my refrigerator, and decided that if things this evening were as they had been, distant, awkward, then I would force the conversation. *Where is this going, Lupita? What am I to you? Do we have a future?* Then of course I imagined my abject misery if she rejected me. What would I do then? I was a jumble of nerves by the time she texted to tell me she was on her way. She arrived wearing her work clothes, her austere gray suit, her hair pulled back in a tight bun. She looked nervous, her face strained. I wondered if her stressful day had continued or if she was as anxious to have the proverbial talk as I was. We hugged and she asked if she could use the bathroom. Minutes later she emerged wearing a different outfit altogether and with her hair down, pulled back but loose.

"Wow," I said. "Where'd you find that?"

"I had a change of clothes in my bag. I went home and had just enough time to grab whatever was around before anyone could ask where I was off to. Always too many people interested in my business."

She now seemed relaxed and happy and warm, different from our last couple of interactions. She looked around my apartment, a wide-eyed expression on her face. She asked questions about a series of photos I had pushpinned to the wall—poorly shot tourist photos I'd taken in San Francisco that, in black and white, I thought were artistic. She picked up books I had stacked on every surface, quickly examining both the front and back covers and then setting them down. She spent a long time examining two yellowed nineteenth-century maps of Mexico that I'd found folded in an old book purchased for six dollars at a yard sale. One of them was from before the 1848 US-Mexican War and included the entire southwest as part of Mexico.

"I like your place," she said.

"Oh?"

I thought maybe she had just said it to say it, something one says automatically, but then she surprised me.

"It reminds me of an old bookshop I remember visiting in my dad's pueblo," she said. "The owner also kept records of deeds and stuff. It was full of books, records, maps, and photographs from around the world. My dad had just gone inside to ask about a piece of land and we took off quickly, but I never forgot the place. I wanted to stay there forever." Then she looked at me and smiled sheepishly, as if she had admitted more than she'd intended. I thought of her distance the last couple of weeks. Had I been wrong? There was nothing distant in that look.

We finished dinner and she cleared the dishes and I told her to leave them in the sink, but she washed them anyway. Lacking a task, I began organizing the kitchenette counters, placing containers and utensils in cabinets and drawers as if I had just that evening taken them out.

When we were through we were both quiet. "Do you need to get home?" I asked her.

I was standing in the middle of the main room and she was in the kitchenette drying her hands. She nodded, but said nothing. Then she walked toward me. She was looking directly into my eyes. "Soon, but not right now," she said, continuing in my direction. I just stood there, unsure whether to step forward or backward or even what to do with my hands. There in the middle of my studio, all I could do was wait for her as she approached with longing eyes. She looked at me just as she had years before when we sat across from one another during PE roll call (only at that moment did I fully recognize the look). Soon she was close enough that she reached out her arms. I thought for a second that she was going to kiss me, her eyes still looking into mine, but she turned her cheek and placed it on my chest, the rest of her head nestled into my neck. She hugged me as if it brought her relief, as if she had been waiting to hug me like that all night. "I'm sorry we haven't been able to see each other much," she said. "My brothers are very protective. And they started to ask me too many questions. They—"

I stopped her. "You don't need to explain," I said. Although an explanation was exactly what I had needed—that day at lunch, our previous outings all so rushed and distant, the last couple of weeks spent worrying that our relationship was doomed.

We kissed gently at first, slowly, but then we kissed harder, and I felt her hand on the back of my head, her fingers grabbing my hair, pulling me toward her. I led her to my bed. She sat on the edge and then leaned backward. I crawled on top of her, fumbling with the buttons of her shirt. My fingers felt thick and clumsy. She lifted off my shirt, and then my undershirt, before I could undo half the buttons. Finally her shirt opened and I pulled it away from her and she removed the rest as if in a hurry, as if she had felt suffocated by it. I unhooked her bra and she pulled it away from herself, quickly covering her breasts with her forearm. She stopped kissing me. "Can you turn off the light?" she said.

44

"What? Really?" I said, disappointed. Her arm only covered her nipples. The rest of her full breasts were visible, and I wanted to see them whole, not just piece by piece.

"But I want to see you," I said.

She shook her head. "No," she said. "Please."

I rose and turned off the light. The room was pitch dark. I decided it was better this way. It had been so long since I'd had sex that I thought I was going to explode upon contact, and a naked Lupita would have ensured that. At least now I could distract myself with thoughts other than her body. But as I made my way back to the bed my eyes adjusted, and I could see her by the dim light of a streetlamp outside my window. My performance was going to be short lived. Then I noticed that she had turned her back toward me and was facing the wall.

"Is everything okay?" I asked.

She was silent.

I reached out to caress her shoulder and she stiffened.

"What's the matter?" I asked. I couldn't believe this was happening again. How long were memories going to keep getting in the way?

"There's something we have to talk about," she said.

"Yes?"

She was quiet for a long time and I heard her sigh deeply. My heart was pounding. I really didn't know what to expect. I thought maybe she was going to bring up Ernie again, or tell me that she was seeing someone else. Then it popped into my mind that maybe she was going to tell me she had herpes, which is a conversation I'd had before with a girl in college. Though disappointing, it was certainly information I was happy to have *prior* to sexual intercourse. But I should've known better.

"You know how I said that my brothers are overprotective?"

"Yeah, I remember. In high school guys used to have to fight them in order to date you, right?"

She was quiet for a moment. "So you know?"

"Know what?"

"That in order to date me you have to fight them."

"You mean, still?"

I saw her nod her head slowly.

"You're lying," I said.

Now she shook her head.

"So for us to be together," I said, my voice rising, "I'm going to have to fight them?"

She turned toward me. In the darkness I couldn't tell exactly what the expression on her face was, but it seemed as though she was just staring at me while I connected the very obvious dots. I suddenly imagined her brothers already outside my door, waiting for me, gnashing their teeth and punching their palms in anticipation.

"What was all that the other night, then?" I asked. "About not asking me to fight anybody or to be your provider or protector."

"I know. I'm sorry. But this isn't about that. This is *their* rule, my brothers', not mine. There's nothing I can do about it. It's my family—"

"The rule is crazy. Look at me—" I held out my skinny arms and stared down at my shirtless torso—"Your brothers would absolutely murder me. It's not even an option."

"I know it's crazy," she said, "but I love my family, and I live in their home—"

"Move out!" I exclaimed. I stopped short of asking her to move in with me.

"It's not that easy. I'd move out and never be able to return. My parents are strict with me. They lost control of my brothers early on. I became their last hope, the good daughter. They are very traditional—"

"But they allow your brothers to govern your life like this?" My voice was almost shrill. I wanted to stop, to calm myself, but I couldn't. "What's the purpose, anyway? What are they afraid is going to happen if they let you date some guy who they *haven't* beaten to a pulp?"

"This isn't easy for me," she said. "I'm the one who's had to live with this. I'm telling you now before we continue any further and grow more attached. If you want to walk away, I don't blame you. I'm sorry for not telling you earlier, and I'm sorry for confusing you the other night. But this is confusing for me too. I like you, I like you a lot. And I don't want this to end." She was quiet for a moment before speaking again. She spoke lower now, her gaze turned downward. "When I was twelve there were these two boys I hung out with. They were just friends from my neighborhood. I don't remember how it happened exactly, but I guess we were just curious and so we would fool around with each other. I trusted them and I didn't think we were doing anything wrong, but then they bragged about it or something, and eventually word got back to my brothers."

"Did you have sex with them?" I asked. I thought of the middle school rumors from long ago. So there was some truth to them.

She looked up at me quizzically, as though my question were preposterous. I'm not sure why I asked for clarification. It just seemed so weird to me that while I was focused on my lunchtime basketball career, others were exploring their nascent libidos.

"No, nothing like that," she mumbled. "Like I said, we were just being curious. Though it's as if we had. Whatever they bragged about made it sound a whole lot worse. Once word spread, it spread fast. When my brothers found out they just about killed them. But the damage was already done. Twelve years old and I already had a reputation for being a slut. It was horrible. My brothers wouldn't let me out of their sight, and to this day, they haven't let up."

We were quiet for a long time after that, both of us unsure what to do next, how to proceed. Lupita carefully put her bra back on, and I felt a pang of disappointment as I caught a last glimpse of her nipple in the darkness. Then she put on her shirt and I turned the light back on. After a while, she rose from the bed, combing through her hair with her fingers. "I should get going," she said.

"I want to be with you," I blurted out. "More than anything else. But I'm—I'm not a fighter, you know that."

"I know," she said.

"What if I just went and talked to them? I mean, I feel as if they'd see me and forgo the fight out of pity."

She laughed gently. "You don't know my brothers. They don't feel sorry for anyone."

She grabbed her bag and walked toward the door. I followed her and she turned toward me and looked into my eyes. I was waiting for her to say, "So I guess I'll be seeing you," but she remained silent, as if she were waiting for me to say the parting words. But I didn't want to say good-bye. It felt preemptive. Our relationship couldn't end because of something so unfathomable, something so incomprehensible.

"What if we just continued," I said, surprised by my boldness. "What if we were just careful? They don't have to know, at least not for—"

She suddenly stepped toward me and reached her arms around my neck and pulled me close. I could feel the warmth of her breath as she whispered into my neck, "Are you sure?"

"Yes," I said, feeling her lips close to my skin.

"Okay, but we're going to have to be extra careful." She kissed my neck, then my cheek. Then she placed her lips over my bottom lip, and I felt myself being pushed back toward the bed. She didn't ask to turn off the light this time. As a result, our lovemaking ended much quicker than I would've liked, but it was just as well because as soon as we were done she gathered her clothes and said, "Now I *really* need to get home!"

After she left I wondered what "extra careful" would entail. But only briefly. My euphoria soon took over, and for the rest of the night I kept smiling to myself and saying, "You just had sex with Lupita Valdez. Who did? You did?" Yes, I did.

CHAPTER THREE

I

AFTER THAT NIGHT, we were together, there was no question. All the awkwardness was gone. We suddenly could hold hands and kiss and think nothing of it. It was natural, comfortable. Seeing each other became expected. Every day after work she would call me and drive out to Davis, even if she didn't have much time. Some days she would arrive, we would make love quickly, and then she would leave. I think at first she felt self-conscious about that—I did too, as I certainly contributed my part to the briefness—but eventually she let her inhibitions go and accepted the idea, if only because that was how things had to be. There were restrictions on our relationship, we both knew that, and yet we didn't talk about it. We just understood. She had to be home because otherwise her brothers would begin asking questions. So it was okay if she just came for a half hour, an hour, and it was okay if all that we wanted to do was make love and lie there naked in each other's arms, recovering for as long as we could before she had to dress and drive back to Woodland. There was something illicit about our relationship that created an urgency to our meetings. Sometimes I wondered: If we had been able to see each other without worry, as much as we wanted, as often as we wanted, would our need for one another have been less? But this was all we knew, and I didn't care to question it too much.

Eventually she grew bolder and stopped worrying that around every corner she was going to run into her brothers. She avoided saying anything directly about fighting them. She was aware that I knew what was at stake. It didn't have to be restated. I didn't need reminders. I was okay with the way things were—at first I was. The predicament was simpler for me. I didn't have to answer anyone's questions. I never had to come up with excuses. She had to constantly. She told her family about friends visiting from out of town, car trouble, work-related trips, some of the excuses so flimsy that I wondered if her brothers really did care as much as she thought they did. Maybe they were just stupid and believed her; maybe they were waiting for her to slip up. All I had to do was stay in my book-strewn apartment in Davis and wait for her. The pressure was never on me, though I guess I was the one being protected. On the days when she wasn't able to get away, she would call and I would wait for the next day, anxious to see her, frustrated, but knowing what the alternative was. Months passed in this way. At times we would leave my studio and go to dinner in downtown Davis. If her excuse allowed her the time we'd go to the movies. We grew more comfortable together, and even gave ourselves over to the occasional embrace or kiss in public.

Then we were almost caught. It was a Friday evening in early March. We had an extra couple of hours that night because she had told her family she would be going out for drinks with her coworkers. After dinner we decided to grab dessert at a café downtown. There were a lot of people out, more than usual because the weather had turned unseasonably warm. Most of them were students, college or high school kids, but there were a good number of families too. The café was brightly lit with yellow walls. We were waiting in a long line, barely able to see the dessert selections behind the glass counter. Lupita stood behind me, her chin resting on my shoulder. I reached behind me and our fingers met, clasping gently. Suddenly her hand drew away and she lifted her chin. She could have been moving for any number of reasons—to move out of someone's path, to get a better look at something across the room—but the abruptness, the instinctive pull away, made me certain that she had seen someone. I didn't turn around. All I heard was Lupita say, "Hello, Joel." I could hear the strain in her voice. I turned around and recognized Joel Gallegos, a friend of Ernie's from high school. He had put on a lot of weight, making him look ten years older than when

I had last seen him. His head was shaved to the skin. He stared at me hard.

"What's going on, Lupita?" he said, still not taking his eyes off of me. He was with a girl as well. She looked to be about seventeen, if that. He didn't introduce her.

"Just getting dessert or something," Lupita said. "How you been?"

Joel didn't answer. He just nodded his head at me. "You look familiar," he said.

I was about to say we had gone to high school together when Lupita cut me off. "He works with me. A friend from work," she said.

We both turned to her.

"That's good," Joel said, as if her answer needed his approval. And that was it. We both turned around, and Joel and the girl went to the back of the line. I felt his eyes on us. Lupita stood a foot away from me, fidgeting nervously and playing with the ends of her hair. When we arrived at the counter I asked her what she wanted—it had been her idea to get dessert in the first place—and she just shook her head distractedly.

"Whatever you want," she said.

I ordered a piece of chocolate cake because I knew she liked chocolate, but once we found a seat she hardly picked up her fork. She waited until Joel and the girl left. Her seat faced away from them, so she didn't have to say good-bye, but she could still see them out of the corner of her eye. On his way out, Joel nodded at me in the same way that Ernie used to, slow and deliberate, but there was something sinister about his nod, as if he was telling me, "I don't know what's going on, but I am going to make it my business to find out."

When they were gone Lupita told me why. Joel was one of Ernie's closest friends after high school. He had always been Ernie's sidekick, never cool enough or tough enough, so he latched on to someone who was and staked everything on that relationship, pretending like it was up to him to preserve his friend's reputation. "But what really sucks," Lupita said, her voice weak, "is Joel works with my brother at Pep Boys. With

Chucho." She had no doubt that Joel would tell Chucho that he'd seen her out with some guy.

I told Lupita not to worry, but of course I knew she had every reason to. My reassurance was empty, especially because I was still focused on the sting of being called a friend from work. I realized that might have been her only chance of playing it off—that is, if he hadn't seen her with her chin on my shoulder—but it bothered me. Once again it was a petty matter of pride, but it still left a bitter taste in my mouth. Maybe it would've disappeared if we had returned to how we were before running into Joel, if she had held my hand or put her arm through mine. Instead she walked at a distance, rigid and cold. I was practically on one side of the sidewalk and she on the other. She was silent, lost in thought. I knew there was nothing to say. We just had to wait and hope that nothing further came from the encounter.

On Monday I didn't hear from her after work. She had texted at lunch and told me that she would call as soon as she was off. It grew late and I started to worry. At first I tried to study, but I couldn't concentrate. I began pacing back and forth in my apartment, imagining different scenarios. Joel probably told her brother, and he in turn told the other two, and the three of them were probably waiting for Lupita when she got off work. If she stood firm and denied it, then they were at least watching her closely, preventing her from calling anyone. She could've sent me a text, I reasoned. It would have been easy to have sent one, gone to the bathroom and written something like, "Don't worry, call tomorrow." Instead I had to wait until after midnight. I was falling asleep. The phone rang and startled me.

She spoke in a whisper and confirmed my fears. Joel had told her brothers, and even though she denied everything, they didn't believe her and demanded to see her phone. Luckily, she always called me from her work cell phone, so all they saw were calls to girlfriends. They checked her texts too, but we hadn't exchanged many, and those were on her work phone as well. They kept her phone anyway. When she demanded it back they asked her why she needed it so badly. She told them that she wasn't a little girl anymore and she could call and hang out with whoever she wanted. They were unequivocal in their response: no, she could not. They alone approved of the people she hung out with. They were her brothers, they protected her. I told Lupita that they sounded insane.

We didn't see each other the next day either, but on Wednesday morning Lupita took the day off of work and headed directly to my place. She called me on the way and told me that she had to see me. She couldn't wait until her brothers looked the other way. They had been awakened and were now extra vigilant. She explained that after Ernie was killed they let up a little, probably because they thought she was still grieving. But now they must've realized that enough time had passed. She wouldn't grieve forever. Maybe she had already moved on. They would now keep closer tabs on her.

I was still in bed when Lupita knocked on my door. It wasn't yet eight thirty. I rose and opened it. She rushed into my arms and immediately burst into sobs. It was raining outside and her hair and clothes were damp. I was still in my boxers and without slippers. The outside air was cold, but I couldn't reach to shut the door without letting go of her. Another tenant, a Korean girl wearing a green rain slicker, passed by outside, eyeing us strangely. I nodded to let her know everything was okay. After a few moments Lupita composed herself and went to the bathroom. I closed the door and put on sweat pants and socks. When she emerged she had let her hair down and changed out of her work clothes. We crawled back into bed and stayed there for hours. We awoke and held one another, saying nothing. She was trembling, and I asked her if she was cold, but she shook her head. She had been truly spooked. It wasn't until then that I realized just how afraid she was of her brothers. Finally, I asked her, "What can we do?" She pulled away and looked at me. I thought she was going to say it: "Fight them." She was, I'm sure of it, the words were on the tip of her tongue. "Fight them and this will be over." But at the last moment she must have changed her mind, because she said, "We'll just have to be more careful."

||

We were discovered again, but this time it was my turn to be caught off guard. On weekend mornings Lupita usually went to the gym, but often she would drive to me instead. Her brothers expected her to be away for an hour or two, and she could hide a change of clothes in her gym bag, so it was a good excuse. Davis was quiet on early weekend mornings, especially on Sundays, and we usually felt safe from running into her brothers' friends, who had probably been out late the night before, or any of her family members, who were probably heading to church. We decided to grab breakfast downtown. It had rained a lot the previous week, but that day it was bright and spring was in full bloom. It was nice to be outside my apartment, to be in public with one another. We'd grown more careful about holding hands or showing affection, so it surprised me that after we finished our meal and were leaving the restaurant, Lupita grabbed my hand and drew close to my side. I tensed for a second, but I decided that if she felt safe enough, then I did as well. I felt a surge of warmth at having her clutch on to me like that. It was the kind of closeness that most couples take for granted, but which I couldn't fathom; that it was so easy, you just held on to your partner without fearing someone was lurking around the corner ready to beat the shit out of you. As the door swung behind us and we passed the tables on the outside patio I heard a familiar voice call out, "Hey!" It sounded like my father. I was sure I was mistaken. Then the same voice called out, "Mijo!" I turned and there were my parents.

They had come into the same restaurant, and I hadn't seen them because my back was to the door. I expected Lupita to draw away, and she did, but not immediately. She must have been as stunned as I was. She said later that she recognized them instantly as my parents, that I was an equal mix of the two.

"Hey, Mom and Dad," I said.

Now Lupita pulled away, slowly, so as not to make it too obvious, but my parents had already noticed. I could see that my father felt embarrassed for me, and since he didn't wish to cause me any further awkwardness, he tried to make light of the situation. He smiled widely, his thick black mustache curving upward. "We were planning on checking up on you afterward," he said. "Your mom wanted to surprise you, but I guess the surprise is on us." He turned to Lupita and nodded, smiling warmly.

"This is Lupita," I said. "Lupita, these are my parents."

Lupita was smiling from ear to ear, her almond-shaped eyes becoming nothing more than narrow slits. I could see her reach to play with the ends of her hair, which she did whenever she was nervous or anxious. She must have been aware of their appraising eyes, eyes looking for a reason why I might not have mentioned this new person in my life. I saw my parents at least once a week, usually for dinner, and although I'd been tempted, I decided not to tell them about Lupita. It was difficult enough for the two of us to hide our relationship. I don't know how word would've ever passed from my parents' circle of friends and acquaintances back to Lupita's brothers, but I didn't want to take the chance. Also, knowing my mom, she would've wanted to be close to Lupita, and that would've complicated matters further. As it was, we said good-bye—my parents gushing, overdoing their expressions of pleasure at having met her—walked back to my place, and parted ways, and already my mother had called. She left a message inviting me to dinner that night. She said nothing about Lupita, but she did mention that if I wanted to bring anybody I was more than welcome. I called back later and told my mom that I would come, but it would just be me. "Oh," she said, the disappointment evident in her voice.

"Well, that girl seemed nice this morning. *Very* pretty, but you know that, I'm sure."

She was baiting me. "Okay, Mom," I said curtly. "I'll see you at seven."

We hung up the phone and suddenly I felt bad—for my parents who naturally just wanted to be included in my life, and for myself at having to decide how to explain my predicament. *So you see, Mom, Dad, there's a slight hitch—yeah, no big deal—just that in order to be with her I have to fight her three brothers.* But telling them was not an option. Like most protective parents of an only child, I knew they would only worry themselves into a manic state. So I would just play down our relationship, tell them that we were taking it slow.

I arrived that evening and both my parents were in the kitchen. My dad was making the salad, and my mom was periodically checking the focaccia in the oven. My parents now lived in a Spanish-style stucco home on Third Street, the same street where I grew up but on a different side of town. I had grown up on the north side, which was just a two-minute drive across Main Street, but the north side was closer to Fourth and Fifth Streets, one of the poorer and sketchier neighborhoods in town. The homes and streets in between varied; some were nice old homes, Victorian and Edwardian era, others were dilapidated tract homes and crowded apartment buildings. Tony Galíndez and I were technically neighbors, but he grew up in a run-down apartment complex next door. Both my parents had been promoted to better-paying positions when I was in high school. They saved and moved into their current home when I was in my sophomore year at college. This house was significantly swankier, something I teased them about—"Your activist years are far behind you now"—but in truth I was happy for them. They both liked to cook and the kitchen had been renovated with not one detail left undone, a mix of modern stainless steel and Mexican tile. I liked the new house, but it never felt like home to me. I sat on one of the wooden stools at the center island. My parents asked me the usual questions about school and I answered them in depth, finding it infinitely easier to answer these questions than to face the obvious one. I got up and set the table in the dining room, lit the candles, and then turned on my parents' usual dinner music, a mix of Latin jazz and classical.

Midway through eating there was a lull in the conversation, the sound of our utensils against our plates growing more prominent. It seemed we had exhausted all possible subjects, and now either I was waiting for them to bring up Lupita, or they were waiting for me to bring her up voluntarily. My father broached the subject first in his lighthearted way.

"That was quite the beauty you were with this morning. What's she doing with you?"

I laughed and waited for a quick response to come to me. In the end I settled for, "Yeah, she is."

My mother wanted to know her name again.

"Lupita," I said.

And from there the questions picked up speed.

"Where did you meet?"

"We've known each other since junior high."

"How did you meet again?"

"We ran into each other."

"Does she go to school?"

"No, she works at Mervyn's."

"What does she do there?"

"She's a manager."

"At the one in town?"

"She's in regional sales, so she works at a few of them."

"I don't remember hearing you talk about her. Did you know each other well in high school?"

"No, we didn't know each other well. I mostly knew of her. She was homecoming queen."

"I could have guessed that," my father chimed in.

Finally, when all the background questions had been asked, restated, and asked again for clarity, my mother asked, "How long have you been seeing each other?"

"A little while," I said quietly.

"A couple of weeks? Months? *Years?*" she asked, a little exasperated at my reticence.

"Months," I said.

"That's what I thought," she said. "You look very comfortable together."

I didn't know what that meant. Comfortable? How in that short glimpse could my mother have surmised that we were comfortable together? In fact, the opposite was true: we were always uncomfortable in public.

"Just out of curiosity," my mother said, "we know you're a grown-up now, and just because you live close by doesn't mean you lose your independence, but why hadn't you told us about her before?"

"There was nothing to tell," I said, unable to hide my irritation. I wanted the questions to stop. "We're taking things slow. I just started school. We want to see how things progress."

After that they dropped the subject.

Later, after we'd cleared the table, my mother excused herself to call my grandmother, which she did every Sunday evening, and my father and I sat on the couches in the living room and watched television. He held the remote and flipped through the channels quickly until he settled on a movie or some television drama. A commercial came on and he lowered the volume. "You know, mijo," he said. "I know you don't want to talk about it anymore, but your mom, after she saw you and Lupita together today, you know what she said? She said that you were in love. She had known that something had changed in your life, but she didn't know what. But now she knew. The instant she saw you guys together."

"What are you talking about?" I said.

He chuckled. "Calm down. I'm just saying, mothers sometimes know. And I have to agree with your mom. Even in that short meeting, I could tell you and her have something special."

I was about to tell him again about taking things slow, but he cut me off.

"I know, I know," he said, raising his hand to gesture that he was making his last point. "I'm just saying don't take things *too* slow." Then he paused and asked, "What does that mean

58

anyway, taking things slow? Sounds to me like a way of avoiding something." His right eyebrow was raised, and underneath his thick mustache I could tell he was smirking.

At that moment I felt as if he could see right through me. I wanted to tell him. Maybe it'd be a relief just to have it off my chest. Maybe he'd even have sober advice. I cleared my throat. "So, let's just say there is something I'm avoiding."

"Oh?" he said. His smile broadened. He rose in his chair and crossed his arms. He appreciated when I brought him into my confidence.

"But you can't tell mom. She'll freak out."

"I swear," he said, and then he made an exaggerated sign of the cross and kissed his fingers.

"I'm serious."

"I know, I can tell," he said. "I promise, it's between you and me."

"Well, the thing is, in order to date Lupita, like actually *be* with her in a relationship, you have to fight her three brothers first."

My dad was silent, and I felt my words hang heavily in the air between us. I was waiting for him to cry out in protest, to rush to my side and reassure me that everything would be okay. I didn't expect him to burst out laughing. He practically roared.

"I'm serious," I said.

"I'll tell you," he managed between guffaws and holding his side. "I didn't expect that. That's a good one!"

"It's not a joke," I said, and I tried to be very solemn so he could see that I was serious, but this had really tickled his fancy and he only laughed harder. When he stopped finally, sighing loudly, he said, "Hell, for a girl that pretty I'd fight her brothers, her father, her uncles, her cousins—" and he counted them off on his thick fingers.

"I know you would," I said. My dad was something of a brawler in his younger days. "I'm talking about me though."

He looked over at me, the sparkle still in his eyes. "Well, what are you pushing, like 140?"

"One forty-five."

"Yeeeeeeah, I'd put on like twenty pounds first." Then he started laughing again until my mom called from the other room, "What's so funny in there?"

"Nothing!" I yelled.

"Our vato loco is off to fight for his ruca," my dad called out.

"Dad, please!"

Then I heard my mother in the other room tell my grandmother over the phone, "They're being silly in there. Yeah, something on TV about vatos or cholos or something. Cholos. CHO-LOWES, you know, like hoodlums."

III

So my dad didn't believe me, but I took his advice anyway. I started going to the gym and lifting weights. It's laughable when I recall the excuses I gave myself for going: I wanted to relieve the stress of school, I spent too many hours sitting at my desk, I wanted to be healthier, I was tired of being a scrawny bookworm. When I just should have said that I wanted to lift weights and get stronger because maybe, just maybe, when the day comes that I have to fight the Valdez brothers, they won't annihilate me. I had access to the university facilities, and after working out alone for several weeks with very little progress, I met a student from Southern California named Ronaldo. He was in the law program. After running into each other several times, we started nodding to one another in greeting. Then he asked me once to spot him while he bench-pressed what looked like an absurdly heavy amount. His brown face turned shades of purple as he struggled to lift the weight. I wouldn't have been much help if he'd dropped it. Other times I asked him questions about certain machines and he was happy to answer in great detail, more detail than I needed or paid attention to. He was a workout fanatic. Short but muscular, his head seemed too large for his body, or his neck too thick, or his arms too long; I don't know, there was just something off about his body, as if he was halfway between a dwarf and someone merely short. He explained later that he had been a wrestler in high school and had probably stunted his growth by lifting weights at too early an age. He said his brothers were all older and he had wanted to be like them, big football guys, but he never grew above their noses. He didn't seem too bitter about it. In fact, I don't think he thought his body structure was abnormal. If anything, he probably thought my body structure was the one to be laughed at: skinny neck, frail arms, no chest to speak of, sticks for legs. I was the portrait of someone who had done very little physical activity in his life.

Maybe he realized I was struggling, because one day he asked if I wanted to join his workout routine. A few days later he brought me a weight-gain supplement, then a protein supplement, and then a creatine supplement, which I questioned but he assured me was safe and natural. Ronaldo seemed happy to have a partner, and his enthusiasm was contagious. Instead of dreading the exercise, feeling it futile and pointless, I suddenly began to see improvements, not just the amount I could lift but actual physical changes—definition in my arms and chest, the discovery of muscles I didn't know I had in my shoulders—and this spurred me on further.

Ronaldo was a fan of WWE, Mexican luchadores, and Ultimate Fighting. He talked about them nonstop. Once he told me about a fight he had seen on television the night before. He described the fighters' physical attributes: one was tall, with a long reach, not particularly muscular, but he was quick; the other was shorter, built low to the ground, and very strong. He explained their fighting strengths: the tall one had a background in kickboxing; the shorter one knew martial arts. Then round by round Ronaldo described each fighter's tactic. The fight ended with the two men locked on the mat exchanging punches at close range, which, of course, worked to the shorter man's favor. I don't know why Ronaldo chose that fight to describe in such detail. Something about it had impressed him, and I found myself listening intently to his retelling. But my interest turned to fear when it dawned on me that all this strength training really was pointless if I didn't know the first thing about how to fight. What good was benching your body weight (which I could now do) if you were knocked out cold with one punch to the jaw?

I toyed with the idea of telling Ronaldo about my predicament. I even daydreamed that he would offer to train me. I could see the two of us hitting punching bags, doing sit-ups, me running around Davis as he rode his bicycle alongside and yelled out words of encouragement. But I only got as far as asking him if he'd ever been in a fight himself. He had, plenty of times, back in high school, and then of course with his brothers. I asked if he'd won the fights. He thought for a moment and gave me a surprisingly accurate answer: "I'd say I'm 10–4, maybe 10–3 and one tie."

"That's a lot of fights," I said.

He didn't seem to think so. "My brothers were in lots more," he said. "They were always fighting, coming home with bloody noses and black eyes, and most of the time laughing as they recounted the blow-by-blow and what they were thinking." He mimicked them, "So I was gonna punch him like this, but then I slipped on something, so then I had to come around the other side and I was thinkin'—" Ronaldo began to laugh. "I guess I did the same the thing too. As soon as a fight is done you think about all the things you could have done, and the things you *did* do; well, you wish you could relive them."

"But don't you fear getting hurt?" I asked.

"No, things only hurt later when the adrenaline wears off. In the fight you don't feel a thing. That's not true. What I mean is, you don't feel it like you would if you were to just slam your hand in the door. Adrenaline is a powerful drug. The human body is an amazing thing. Imagine that? In order for you to survive, the body has a chemical that keeps you going, distracts you from your pain. No, the worst part about fighting, especially if you win, is the fear of retribution. You never know when someone is going to retaliate. Most of the time they don't, but it's the constant looking over your shoulder or wondering if you should go to this particular party because this person might be there, or even friends of that person who might hold a grudge. That's no fun. That's when the fight extends into the day-to-day, and for me it's not worth it. If it was one fight and then over with right then and there, then maybe, but when it has no foreseeable end it's not worth it, it's pointless."

I would only have to fight the Valdez brothers once, I thought. Once and it'd be done, behind me. And as far as looking over my shoulder, that was the result of not fighting. I asked Ronaldo if he had ever fought three people at the same time. He laughed. "That's a funny question," he said. "No, but I've been jumped by four people—I don't know if that qualifies exactly as a fight. I just covered my head and rolled up into a ball until they had their fill."

I wondered if that would have to be my tactic. He must have wondered why I was asking so many questions, because he asked, "How come, you thinking about fighting someone?" He had a strange smile on his face, as if the idea excited him.

"No, I'm just curious," I told him. Then I explained that I had never been in a fight before and I didn't think I was capable of it.

Ronaldo grew serious, as though he was concerned that I had such a low estimation of myself. "Everyone is capable," he said. "What matters is the fight inside. You just have to keep in mind that you're not going to die—bones heal, flesh heals, but it's very hard to die."

I wondered if this was true. Even so, it didn't make me feel any better.

CHAPTER FOUR

I

SEVERAL MONTHS PASSED in the same way. Lupita and I saw each other less regularly, but even that took on a certain routine. If we agreed to meet after work and she didn't show, I would assume that her brothers had grown suspicious and decided to hold her up. They would make her cook for them. They would ask her to accompany them to visit friends or family. They would sit on the front porch and make her sit with them and listen to their asinine conversation. So I would wait for a whispered call, a brief text, or an apologetic phone call the next morning explaining why she wasn't able to get away. This was the norm. We were used to it, or at least I was. Every now and then she would groan and say something about wishing we didn't have to sneak around, and I would wonder if she was hinting that if I just fought them all of our troubles would go away. Of course, she was just expressing a desire to see one another freely, something I desired as well, but I couldn't help but interpret it as a wish that I would take matters into my own hands and deal with this obstacle once and for all.

Soon it was May, almost the end of my second year in graduate school. One morning Lupita called and excitedly told me that she had a work retreat the coming weekend in Monterrey and that her coworker couldn't make it, so she had the room to herself. "Other than the workshops during the day," she said, "we can have a weekend to ourselves at the beach." When we hung up the phone I could hardly contain myself. I whistled while I packed.

On Friday Lupita picked me up at my apartment after work and we drove toward the coast. The drive was long and we hit traffic, but we didn't mind. Nothing else existed; we were free, her brothers were miles away, there was no chance of running into anyone, and she had an excuse for the entire weekend. It was just the two of us and that was all that mattered. At one point I said, "What if we just didn't go back? What if we just drove somewhere and decided to stay? There are Mervyn's everywhere; you could transfer."

She laughed. "And your classes?" she asked.

"Forget them. I'd transfer too."

"And your family?" she asked.

"They'd come and visit."

"And mine?"

"Well, your parents could come and visit as long as they don't tell your brothers."

We laughed, but at the mention of her brothers it stopped being so funny. It was like that. The unsaid could be ignored; once said, it filled the room (in this case, the car). By the time we arrived she had to meet coworkers for a cocktail mixer. I stayed in the room and watched television until I shut it off so I could listen to the waves. I fell asleep imagining us walking together on the beach. She woke me up sometime that night, removing my shirt and hers, then my pants, and we made love.

We woke up early and walked along the beach, empty save for a few other people walking and some surfers in wetsuits. It was cold and overcast, but that didn't take away from the beauty of the sea and the distant cliffs emerging from the fog. We held hands as we walked the entire span of the beach and back, hardly talking. We were hungry when we returned, and we went in search of a diner before she had to get back for her first training session. We ended up grabbing coffee and pastries at a café. When she left to meet her coworkers, I stayed in the hotel room and watched television until I fell asleep again, tired from not having slept much the night before. At four thirty Lupita called and told me she'd be back soon, a half hour or so. I was anxious to see her and the minutes passed slowly. I hadn't been bored during the day. I had brought some books to study, but I had mostly watched television, enjoying the mindlessness of it. Expecting her to walk in the door any second, I placed my books in my bag and straightened out the bed and even fluffed the pillows. Then I just sat there and waited, and the time continued to drag until finally I heard the key card slide and a gentle knock. I stood up from the chair and watched as she shut the door and set down her purse along with a new canvas bag they must have given her at the workshop.

"Hello," she said, her voice tired. She stepped into the bathroom before I could see her in the light.

"What have you been doing all day?" she asked from the bathroom.

"Nothing really, just reading. How about you?"

"Just a second," she said as she closed the door.

I sat back down in the chair and waited for her. I felt a strange desperation. I longed to see her face, and here she was just in the other room. I heard the sink turn on and then off. Then the door opened and I could see the bathroom light hit the dark entryway. I rose quickly and walked toward her and came around the corner just as she was entering the hall area. I startled her and she yelped, but I quickly put my arms around her waist and she put her arms around my neck and we kissed. I drew away and looked at her. "I missed you," I said. "I missed you too," she said, but I knew she meant for that day while she was at the conference, and I tried to explain that I missed her from one moment to the next, even when she was in the next room, even when she was asleep, but then I gave up as she covered my mouth with hers.

That night I asked her. We were lying in bed, and all I could think was how I wanted nothing more in life than this, for us just to be together. And not just for a day or for a weekend getaway. I wanted to be with Lupita always. I wanted to have children with her. I wanted us to have a life together, and I couldn't explain it except in these absolutes, and when it came to forever, our entire lives, this one fight seemed insignificant. It was just something I had to do. "Do you want me to fight your brothers?" I asked.

Lupita paused for a long time, not looking my way. Then she said to me, her voice calm, resigned, "If you do they'll leave us alone."

"And what if I don't?"

"They'll never go away. They'll always be there. I wish it was different, I wish there was another way, but they are who they are and they'll never change."

"Okay," I said. "I'll do it."

I half expected her to cry out, "No!" Instead she was silent. So silent I thought maybe she didn't hear me.

I repeated myself.

"I heard you," she said, and she patted my chest. I don't think she believed me, which was just as well. I couldn't just say I was going to fight them. I had to do it.

School ended and over the summer I did research on campus for one of my professors. I spent most of my days in the library, photocopying old magazines and journals, cataloging articles about José Martí, the Cuban poet and revolutionary, and his influence on Mexican intellectuals in the late nineteenth and early twentieth centuries. After our weekend away and my promise to fight her brothers, Lupita and I didn't talk about it again. We easily returned to our routine, seeing each other when we could, and I lost some of my resolve. I began having dreams of fighting, and in every dream my wrists buckled upon contact. My punches were worthless, like a little boy play-boxing with his father. I didn't know my opponent, I never saw his face. I just knew there was a confrontation and fierce movement, and when I struck out to defend myself all I had were limp fists. One day, as we were working out, I mentioned it to Ronaldo. He told me that ineffectiveness in dreams wasn't uncommon, and I wondered how he knew this. Did he have similar dreams? He told me he did not have that dream specifically, but he had never had a dream where he was anything *but* ineffective. Hearing this made me feel better, but not much. Later, when walking through the dim corridors of the library stacks, I tried to imagine the fight, but it was the same as in my dreams, just movement and faceless figures. It was the faceless-ness that terrified me most. I realized I didn't know what the Valdez brothers looked like anymore. The younger two, Eddie and Frankie, I remembered from high school, but I imagined they had changed. I was suddenly curious to see them, to know, at least, whom I was going to have to fight. Maybe seeing their faces would humanize them, remind me that they weren't phantoms but simply men.

One afternoon, after stopping by my parents' house to pick up a book I'd forgotten, I decided to drive by Lupita's. I knew the street, and she had once described her house in detail. I was pretty sure I knew which one it was. It wasn't too far from my old house on Third Street. Her house was a small one-story Craftsman built in the 1930s. The white paint was crumbling and the trim was a faded green. The porch sagged. The yard was well groomed (thanks to her father, she told me; her brothers hardly lifted a finger) and shaded by a large oak tree. Any doubt that it was hers was removed when I saw her brother Chucho's green 1983 Oldsmobile Cutlass in the driveway on blocks. According to Lupita, it was his never-ending hobby. I noticed the car's green sparkly body before I noticed Chucho emerging from underneath the car. He wore a grease-stained, oversized T-shirt. I couldn't tell whether he was fat or muscular, because his shirt hung loosely and made him appear like a hulking mass. The arms of his shirt had been cut off, revealing tattooed biceps and triceps the size of my thighs. In an instant, I decided he was both fat and muscular, but that hardly mattered; what made me weak as I drove back to Davis was the snarl on his face, the look of absolute disgust. He may have just been looking in my general direction, but as soon as I saw his face I turned and stared straight ahead of me. Cars passed all the time, I told myself; there was no reason why he would have registered my face. He didn't know me from anyone.

After that I stayed away for a couple of weeks, but then some dark curiosity compelled me to drive by again. I now wanted to know what the other brothers looked like too. Were they as mean looking? As formidable? I drove by, this time late in the afternoon, and there were the three of them: Chucho on his cell phone in the front walkway, Frankie and Eddie sitting on the porch with beer cans in hand. Lupita's father was there too, sitting next to them on a faded brown recliner. He had a black mustache and was balding, thin strands combed over, just as Lupita had described him. In my brief glance I didn't see any resemblance to Lupita. None of the brothers resembled her either, making it even harder for me to believe that she was a part of this family. One night she had described her parents, her grandmother who was still alive, and her grandfather whom she barely remembered. She told me she looked like her mother. "Exactly like her," she explained, "except thinner. The same eyes, the same facial structure, we laugh alike too." She had described other family members as well, practically everyone except her brothers, circumventing them as if they didn't exist. But now I saw them. The younger two looked liked they did in high school, except bigger—everyone got bigger, just not me, like I was missing some hormone that turned boys into men—and now that I knew what they looked like my fear became even more acute. I preferred the faceless blobs of my dreams. Now the figures smothering the life out of me not only had faces, but goatees, fat jowls, shaved heads, and eyes containing pure hatred for whoever happened to drive by. Why did they need to stare so disgustedly at every car that passed, as if they owned the street?

Weeks passed, and again I mustered up the courage to drive by. I kept hoping for a breakthrough, but my fear only swelled. I waited a month, until the middle of August, and I went again, not knowing what I was doing, telling myself that if I was going to fight them I at least needed to scope out the scene and plan my approach. But the more I drove by and the more time that passed, the more I began to realize that I wouldn't be able to fight them. Ever. It was the most unnatural thing I could imagine, like driving smoothly down the road and suddenly veering off and slamming into a telephone pole: the insane thought may cross your mind, but the thought alone is enough to curb the impulse.

One day I drove by Lupita's house, forgetting that the previous night she had texted me to say she wasn't feeling well and might stay home. That morning I helped my dad move a couch. Before heading back to Davis I decided to make a detour down her street. I saw Eddie and Chucho standing in the walkway, both of them wearing Raiders jerseys and talking on cell phones. Then my eyes followed the path up to the front steps and I saw Lupita's father wearing a threadbare white T-shirt, sitting and smoking a cigarette, looking tired. My eyes continued up the steps to the front porch and there, instead of Frankie in his usual spot, was Lupita, sitting in the recliner, a colorfully knit blanket wrapped around her shoulders. Even from a distance she looked sick.

She saw me and rose slightly in her chair, the weariness in her face instantly transforming into a morbid fear, as if she expected me to stop and challenge her brothers right then and there. I looked away and drove on, feeling stupid, feeling as if I'd been caught in some pathetic act, something to be ashamed of, though I couldn't say exactly what I'd done. I imagined her point of view; I tried to imagine the expression on my face. What did I look like as I passed by on this test of mine? Was that why I drove by her house every couple of weeks? Was it a test to see if I would ever get closer than the safety of my car driving by at fifteen miles per hour?

She was sick for a couple more days and I didn't hear from her, except for a few text messages saying she still wasn't feeling well. I wanted to see her. I missed her, of course, but I also needed to get past the shame I'd felt after seeing her on the front porch. I didn't want her to keep rehashing that image in her mind, the image of a coward. I decided that's how I must have looked. After two more days without hearing from her, I was certain something was wrong. I needed to see her. I couldn't wait any longer. It was a Thursday, a day I knew her father and brothers were all at work, at least for the morning, and even if they came home I could just say I was a friend from Mervyn's and wanted to check on her. When I drove up to the house I was relieved to find no one in front. I parked across the street from their neighbor's house. For a second, I lost my nerve and considered starting up the car again and driving off. But my desire to see her was greater than my anxiety. I got out of the car and walked up the cement path to her house. I half expected one of the brothers to surprise me, to pop up from behind the '83 Cutlass. What would I do then? Pretend like I had the wrong house? I knocked on the screen door and waited. The door opened, and a woman with a striking resemblance to Lupita appeared. It was her, just older, a little plumper. I studied her face for a moment, stunned; the same golden skin, almond-shaped eyes, and perfectly shaped full lips. "Yes?" she asked. I hesitated, trying to remember the excuse I had prepared beforehand.

"I'm, uh, a friend of Lupita's from work, and I just came by to see how she was feeling," I said. My excuse felt ridiculous. What friend from work would come on a Thursday morning to check on a sick coworker? Especially one as jumpy as me. Her mother invited me in. I entered hesitantly. The house was dark and cluttered with furniture. There were family pictures on the wall and a large cross above the television. It was a small house for six people. I smelled fried food. Lupita's mother told me to sit down and pointed toward the living room. There were two pink plastic laundry baskets piled high with clothes on the couch. I remained standing, and her mother walked down the short hallway and knocked on a door.

"Lupita!" she called out.

I heard Lupita's voice.

"A friend has come to see you," her mother said. She again told me to have a seat, and I found a spot on the arm of the couch. She asked if I wanted coffee or tea. I told her I was fine. A minute later, Lupita emerged from her bedroom, wearing an old beige robe. I had never seen her look so disheveled. She didn't smile. She didn't even look surprised to see me. Her face was cold. So cold she looked ugly. She moved one of the laundry baskets and sat down on the sofa close to the couch where I was sitting.

"How are you feeling?" I asked.

She didn't answer. She just stared at me for a moment. Then she asked, "Why did you come?" The iciness in her voice was alarming. It was almost hostile.

"I had to see you," I said. "I missed you."

She didn't look at me. I felt as if I was dealing with an utterly different person. I didn't know this Lupita. I hadn't even seen the slightest shade of this part of her.

"Maybe I shouldn't have come," I said.

She shook her head and crossed her arms. "No, it's good that you did. We need to talk." She leaned forward and peered into the other room to make sure her mother wasn't around. "I can't see you anymore," she said.

That was all. I waited for her to elaborate, but she just pursed her lips and stared off into the distance.

"What are you talking about?" I asked, my heart pounding in my chest, pounding so loud I felt I could hear it. I was sure she could hear it too. If she did, she was unmoved.

"I just don't think we can continue like this," she said.

"Like what?" I asked. "I told you I would fight them. I just need time." My voice rose and she placed her finger to her lips to shush me. Again she leaned forward and peered around the corner to make sure her mother hadn't emerged from the kitchen.

"It's not that," she said. "I just don't think we can make it work."

"What are you talking about?" I asked. "Why this, why all of a sudden?" My voice was weak. I was ready to burst into sobs, but I knew I would never be able to live with myself if I did. Fortunately, my confusion was greater than my pain. I couldn't make sense of it. I couldn't have imagined she was capable of this. "What's going on?" I insisted. "Tell me!"

But she just repeated herself, reiterating the same thing—I don't think we can make this work, I don't think it's working out, I just don't know where this is going—as if this gave me any more information. Soon her mother came into the room, asked if Lupita wanted anything more, and said she'd be in the backyard watering the flowers. Then she puttered around, slowly straightened a blanket, then picked up a blouse and placed it on top of a load of clothing. Her obliviousness exasperated me. I wanted to scream at her to hurry up. When her mother finally left the room and we heard the back door close, I pleaded with Lupita to tell me what the hell was going on. I was angry now. But she didn't budge; the cold, impassive look in her face was impenetrable. She had transformed herself into a stranger. I had never experienced such a thing. I had never met anyone who could become so different that you didn't recognize them, that no matter what you said or did they wouldn't break.

"This is so fucked up," I said.

She merely raised her eyebrows, as if she disapproved of my language. I stood up abruptly, as if I intended to go somewhere. "Please tell me what's going on or else—"

"Or else what?" she said.

Was she mocking me? I shook my head, still not able to comprehend what was happening. "So this is it?" I said. "I just leave and we go our separate ways?"

She nodded. "I'm sorry. I wish it could be different, but it can't. I wish you the best."

This last part infuriated me: such a meaningless thing to say, wishing me the best, as if we were acquaintances passing on the street. She should have said that the first time we met in the mall and let me go on my way. I didn't say anything else. I didn't even want to look at her, this hideous version of the girl I loved. I just walked to the door, opened it, stepped outside, and thought about slamming it behind me as hard as I possibly could. I wanted to break it. I decided not to. What would I have gained? I shut the door gently, holding on to the knob before it locked, hesitating before letting go. What if I opened the door? I thought. Would she still be distant? Maybe I would open it and she would be sobbing, regretting what she'd done, and I'd know it was her again, my Lupita, the Lupita I loved and who loved me. I couldn't believe this was it. It couldn't end like this. But I let go of the doorknob, and I heard the lock click into place. There was no going back in. Then the screen door slammed shut. I turned slowly and walked down the steps, hoping to hear the door swing open behind me. I drove home wanting to scream.

II

And so that was how it ended, brief and unexpected and without explanation. I had *just* gone to her house for the first time! Otherwise, how long until she would have ended it? I called her but she never picked up. Once a man's voice answered and I hung up. Then immediately afterward her number kept calling, but I ignored it, assuming it was one of her brothers. Then the man left a message asking me to please stop calling him. It wasn't one of her brothers. Apparently she had changed her number and it had been given to someone else. I went to Mervyn's and waited for her, but I never made it farther than the parking lot. I wasn't able to bring myself to confront her and demand that she talk to me, so I could only guess at what might have happened. I ran through the possibilities over and over, every waking hour for days on end. Maybe her brothers found out about us and threatened to kill me. That was the easiest reason to accept: she had done it to save me from harm. Maybe when she saw me drive by—my pathetic attempt at snooping— she knew that I would never fight them and that it was pointless to go on like this. As hard as it was to admit, Lupita wanted me to fight them. It was the only way, she had said. But was it? Couldn't there have been some alternative? Couldn't she have found the courage to face her brothers, told them that she was a grown woman and didn't need their protection?

I thought constantly about her coldness the last time we saw each other, her absolute detachment when she told me it was over. I would picture her face and wonder if she just stopped loving me. It happens, I told myself, but even then she wouldn't have wanted to hurt me like this, she would have at least cared for me as a friend, as someone who had shared a part of her life. She would have let me down easier, with some explanation, even of the "It's not you, it's me" variety. Why did she feel the need to shut me out so absolutely?

My days were miserable. I woke up in the morning, briefly forgetting my desolation, but then it would rush over me and not leave until I fell asleep again that night. My friends from classes, my parents, everyone noticed something was wrong. I could hardly hold a conversation without my mind wandering off to think of Lupita. My mother called me every evening. I only picked up sometimes. She wanted to know what had happened, and I wanted to tell her, but I couldn't. At that point I couldn't tell anyone. It was too difficult to think about, let alone recount for someone else. I just told her, "Things didn't work out between Lupita and me, and it's been hard." And she would ask question after question, but I wouldn't budge. I waited for Lupita's phone call. Every time I answered the phone I expected it to be her. I kept thinking that maybe she'd show up at my apartment after work, repentant, begging for forgiveness. Just in case, I always made sure to be home in the late afternoon, from four until six o'clock, anxiously awaiting her delicate knock.

I still had my research at the library. At first I could barely bring myself to go, but eventually I found that at the very least it was a distraction, even if it was a poor one. For a few hours a day I focused on reading articles, making copies, and then making notations on those copies—everything I could possibly find on José Martí. I met with the professor, Joseph Kingman, every Wednesday at his office to give him my research and notes. We usually spoke briefly about the work and that was it. But a few weeks before the end of summer break, Professor Kingman asked me to have lunch with him. As we walked across campus, dodging bicycles left and right, he did most of the talking, telling me about his two young boys—Dexter and Peter—who were going to be starting soccer that fall. My mind wandered to thoughts of Lupita. At some point he asked what the approaching term looked like for me. I hadn't even thought about it, and I told him so. The days dragged by so interminably that a few weeks felt like months away. And then I surprised myself. "I might need to take next term off," I said. I hadn't really thought about it until then, but as soon as I'd said it, I knew that was what I needed to do.

"That would be a pity," he said. "Everything okay with your health? Things at home?"

"I'm fine," I answered. "I just need the break, I guess."

He didn't respond, and we were both silent as we walked across the sunny quad. I wondered if he regretted having asked me to lunch. My misery felt palpable enough to depress everyone around me.

Out of the corner of my eye, I looked at Professor Kingman and examined him from head to toe. He was wearing comfortable-looking loafers, corduroy pants, and a striped collared shirt in need of ironing. He had a thin face with a beak nose, on which rested wire-rimmed glasses. He was balding. I wondered if someday I would be a variation of Professor Kingman. The thought scared me, though not because I felt bad for him. I assumed he led a good life; he seemed satisfied with academia. He lived for his research, his teaching, and his family. But something was lacking in his life that I was sure to lack as well: a burning individuality. Lupita had changed that fact. She had set me apart. Now I was like my colleagues again, no fight hanging over my head, literally or figuratively. Before I had resented the obstacle, but now I *wanted* the fight looming over me, if only because Lupita would still be in my life. I would go home and she'd be waiting outside my studio, wearing her work suit, her hair pulled back, a change of clothes in her bag. I could look forward to the sight of her naked body in my bed. She alone had given worth to everything I did. Only now that she was gone did I realize this. Because everything felt worthless, everything I did, down to the simplest task. Once again I was adrift, but now I knew how it felt not to be.

Professor Kingman began speaking about life as an academic. In his mind I was having doubts about the program, and he wanted to help. I was surprised how closely his words mirrored my thoughts.

"Do you know why I chose José Martí as the focus of my scholarship?" he asked.

I waited for his answer.

"Because he was an intellectual who inspired a country to fight for its independence," he continued. "But he wasn't satisfied merely inspiring with words, for he had been inspired as well and wished to act on that inspiration. His most important function was as a thinker, as a man of ideas, but he needed to do more. And so when the time came he picked up arms and fought against the Spaniards. He was killed in one of the earliest battles. There's a passage in one of his letters where he describes his excitement at being a part of the action. Here he was, almost gleeful to be tromping through the jungle, shooting guns, wanting to be the exact opposite of what he had been all his life—a thinking man, an artist. When I read this for this first time I identified with him, with that moment of excitement. I chose a career in academia because I wanted to be a scholar, respected for my mind, but I think there's a part of every man that wishes to be respected for his valor, his courage, his strength, and so often a man's mind and his strength are seen separately, so that you can't help but feel . . . what would the word be . . . lacking, I guess. Lacking. Do you know what I mean? And Martí, he was no different. One of the most brilliant men in the Americas, and yet deep down he wanted to be seen as someone who could defend the honor of his patrimony, not just through the pen but through the sword."

"Why do you think there's that need?" I asked, almost excitedly.

Professor Kingman shook his head. "The history of the world, men as hunters, men as warriors, men as protectors and providers. How can one escape it? We are all slaves to expectations, real or imagined. All too often we hear from the self-loathing artist or intellectual—self-loathing as a way of dismissing these expectations before others can make the criticism. As if because he's aware of his neurosis and ineptitude it means they don't bother him, but that's not true at all. They do bother you. Everyone wants to be self-assured, and truthfully that doesn't come unless one embodies a certain masculine ideal, probably passed on to us through our fathers, and let's face it, how many ever do? Did our fathers even? So we live our lives laughing at our insecurities, pretending to be smug about them because we're superior in other ways, when deep down we wish we were the bully rather than the bullied, the revolutionary rather than the architect. If José Martí felt this, how can we not help but feel it too?"

I felt very close to Professor Kingman at that moment. I had never had a conversation like this before. He was speaking to me. Maybe he would understand my dilemma. I was not a fighter and so I had lost Lupita, and unless I did something about it I would always be lacking, this failure would always dog me. I decided to tell him. I described the entire situation. I even told him about the inescapable presence of Ernie Rocha. I even tried to describe how in high school being tough meant being Mexican, and being Mexican meant being tough, which left me—an undersized half-breed—really confused. But then I stopped. He had started fidgeting and looking at his watch. It dawned on me that this wasn't what he had in mind when he started telling me about José Martí. He was strictly speaking academically. He was trying to tell me that I needed to find a subject that fascinated me; that not only satisfied my intellectual pursuits, but also touched me spiritually, or else my scholarship would all just be drudgery. I don't think he had the slightest clue how to respond to my situation. His face was pale and he looked stunned. He kept fixing his glasses on his nose, taking them off to wipe them, then putting them on again. He managed nothing more in response than "Hmmm, that's very interesting," "Oh, wow, oh, gosh," and "That's difficult for sure." I waited for more, but he seemed flustered to think that I was asking for personal advice. I quickly steered the conversation back to our research.

I took a leave of absence that term. I couldn't bring myself to go to school, even though at the very least it would have been a distraction. In truth, I didn't want to be distracted. At first I tried to drink away my sorrows. I went to Zitios Bar in Woodland, which I'd been to a few times with Tony Galíndez after we turned twenty-one. I don't know why I drove all the way to Woodland only to have to take a cab back to Davis and then back again the next day to pick up my car. I guess the place better suited my mood. Old drunks and workers in grubby clothes and dudes who just wanted to play pool or watch football. I ordered hard liquor, tequila mostly, on the rocks so that I could at least sip it, and I put the saddest Mexican songs on the jukebox, songs my dad listened to on Sunday mornings. This annoyed the guys who wanted to watch the game, but the old drunks encouraged me, including a man everyone called La Zorra, who would let out a grito at the beginning of every song and then curse the wife who left him for his best friend. I couldn't have found that in Davis. But this routine got old quickly. I tired of the cab rides back and forth to Woodland, which, in addition to my bar tabs, didn't take long to add up. I tried going to a bar in Davis, but the collegial atmosphere, the joviality, the idea that everyone there was drinking to have fun almost made me angry. Their smiles were an insult. I resented their laughter, their easy conversation. I left after one drink. But more than anything, I grew tired of the hangovers every morning, the splitting headaches and the nausea that lasted well into the day, and so after a few weeks I changed course. I decided that I didn't want my thoughts clouded by alcohol and its lingering effects, nor did I want the brief moments of drunken elation or feelings of camaraderie, like when La Zorra put his arm around my shoulder and cried, "A la madre, cabrón!" and then insisted I say it too. I preferred to mope alone. So I walked the streets of Davis, stone sober and completely absorbed in my depression. I sat in coffee shops, drove hundreds of times around Woodland, sat in the Denny's on East Street one day and then the Denny's on Main Street on another, pretending to read a newspaper.

I discovered a point of misery where I actually craved it. I didn't want to forget. All along I rehashed my relationship with Lupita. I engaged in a never-ending, repetitive conversation with her where nothing was ever resolved. At times I imagined what my life would be like if we'd never run into each other that day in the mall, but for the most part I felt deserving of where I was. I was the coward. Never once did I blame her. I dreamed of fighting her brothers, and in my dreams I was no longer ineffective, I was no longer the victim of a swarm of massive bodies falling on top of me, restraining me—now I was the aggressor. I remembered a kid from junior high, a black kid named Augie; he used to fight all the time, and he was a good fighter too, but he fought with so much emotion that he couldn't help but cry as he lashed out at his opponent. He would sob, choked, as if having an asthma attack, and he would fight hysterically, arms and legs flailing, which made other kids afraid of him. Who wanted to fight someone who had lost control? In my dreams I fought like him. I fought with uncontrollable anger, as if I cared about nothing else, or wished for death, or needed to be beaten and maimed, if only for relief. But this was only during my dreams. When awake, or at least sober and rational, I couldn't imagine it. I couldn't ever see this fight, and Lupita always seemed impossibly far away. She was right to end our relationship. If fighting her brothers was what it took to be with her, then I didn't have it in me.

My parents were worried. When I told them I'd taken leave from school, they couldn't understand. They demanded to know more about what was going on in my life. They suggested I see a psychiatrist. I told them I was just heartbroken, so what else was there to do except wait for time to heal my wounds? They wanted to know more about my relationship with Lupita. They wanted to know why I had hidden it from them, why I had never brought her to the house? And so one night at dinner I gave in and told them. I was tired of answering these endless questions. I told them that in order to have a relationship with Lupita, I had to fight her three brothers. I knew they never expected that. All the usual parent advice they had prepared for me was suddenly chucked out the window.

"So you weren't joking, then?" my dad asked.

"You knew about this?" my mom asked shrilly.

My dad looked very concerned, as though just now recalling his fit of laughter. "I guess I did," he said.

My mother, her face pale, asked, "Why do they have to beat up their sister's boyfriends?"

I sighed. "They're just overprotective," I said. "They want to make sure their sister is with someone who can protect her."

"From what?" my mother asked.

I could tell she was horrified. Whatever image she had of Lupita was now changed. Lupita was someone who placed her darling son in danger, and for what? Just so he could be with her? My mother continued, her tone imploring, "But why would she, if she loved you, why would she tolerate this?"

"It's her family, Mom. Just the way her brothers are. If I didn't fight them, I would have to deal with them for as long as we were together. If I fought them, they would embrace me as a brother, they would know that I would do anything to be with their sister."

"Are they big guys?" my father interjected.

I told them they were, and my mom asked incredulously, "What does it even matter? Small guys or big guys, what is proven by fighting? That won't make you a better provider, a more giving lover. There are many ways of protecting those you love other than violence. Can't they see that?"

"Of course," I said, "but that's not the point. The point is they've always had this requirement, and so it's not about the logic behind it, it's just the way it is." I felt as if I were defending the Valdez brothers.

"And her parents support this?" my mother asked.

"I don't know," I said. "I don't think they really have a say. Her brothers have always done what they wanted."

"Well, it is probably better that this person is out of your life," my mother said. "I know you were in love, but this just does not sound like a good situation for you. You don't need to involve yourself with those kinds of people."

My face flushed with anger. I knew what she meant, and I

had often thought the same thing. But I still couldn't help but feel protective of Lupita. "She's not like them," I responded. "If anything, she broke up with me because she wanted to protect me."

"Do you know that for sure?" my mother asked.

I felt a sharp pain in my chest. She had hit me where I was most sensitive.

"I don't," I said. "It's the only thing I can think of. I know she loves me."

My father remained strangely quiet. As my mother carried on, worrying retroactively for the danger I had been in, in disbelief that her son would be caught up in such a mess, and relieved that I was now safe, my father sat with his arms crossed, his pensive face illuminated by the candle flickering on his side of the table. When my mother left the dining room to retrieve something in the kitchen, he asked in a low voice, "What would happen if you were to fight them now? Would she come back to you?"

I shook my head. "I have no idea," I said.

III

It was Tony Galíndez who finally brought some clarity to the situation. I don't know why I went to him. I don't know what I expected him to say. I think I really just wanted to tell someone and have it off my chest.

"*You're* the one seeing Lupita Valdez?" he said, his eyebrows raised, a smile on his face. I almost thought he was excited for me. We were at his apartment, and Tony was on the couch watching television, as he always was during the cannery's off-season. He was shirtless, revealing his hairy chest and the rolls in his stomach. The apartment was stuffy, and he had a fan placed directly in front of him. He moved it when I sat down and changed it to swivel so that the air reached me as well. The room was dark except for the television and the light coming from the kitchen.

"I was," I said. "Not anymore."

"*You're* the one seeing Lupita Valdez?" he asked again, but this time his smile had turned maniacal. He then proceeded to list, in order, counting off on his fingers, all the boys, all the vatos, all the cholos, all the poor fuckers who had tried to date her.

"How is this helping me?" I asked.

"Oh my God!" Tony cried. He was wearing an A's cap, which he removed and tossed on the couch. He rubbed his face with his hands and then stared at me disapprovingly. "You're clueless, aren't you?" he said. "The Valdez brothers heard that Lupita had been dating someone behind their backs, and word was they were looking for that fool, and once they found him they were going to beat the sheeeeee-it out of him. Little did I know that fucker was you!"

I swallowed hard. I had considered this very possibility. My palms were sweaty and I wiped them against my jeans. "They found out she was dating someone?"

Tony shook his head, "My God, I can't believe this! How the hell were *you*, of all people, dating Lupita Valdez?" Then he got quiet and drew closer. "You fuck her?"

I ignored his question and gave a brief rundown of our relationship. When I finished he asked again. "So you fucked her?"

Out of nowhere, I started to cry. I tried to suppress it, but the tears fell anyway, and soon I was sniffling and choking back sobs. His lurid question reminded me that there was a time not too long ago when I actually had made love to Lupita, and on a routine basis. It was painful to think that I would never be close to her again.

Tony was unmoved. "Dude, be thankful your ass is alive. You should be thanking Lupita for breaking up with you. She saved your life! Those bastards would've beat you down. I heard those motherfuckers were pissed when they found out she was dating some dude behind their backs!"

"How did they find out?" I asked.

"Shit if I know. It's Woodland, man, and Davis ain't too far away. You act like you was having your affair back in

Connecticut! Man, seriously, shrug it off. That's one fine-ass notch in your belt. I wouldn't even worry about it."

"What are you talking about?" I shouted. "I was in love with her. My heart is broken."

Tony started laughing. "Calm down, bro," he said, reaching out to place his hand on my shoulder. "Look, hear me out. It's like in the fairy tales, where there's a princess locked up in the tower and she's guarded by a whole series of obstacles, you know what I'm saying?"

I wiped my eyes on my sleeve. "What does that have to do with anything, Tony? Honestly—"

"Let me finish what I'm saying. There's the fortress for one, fool, then the fire pits, the dragon is worst of all, and then even if you get past all that then you gotta answer all the riddles. And so by the end you get there, but unlike the knight whose only purpose on earth is to slay dragons and rescue princesses, you have much more going on in your life. So maybe you get through all those obstacles, or maybe you get through half of them—but what I'm saying is at some point you have to ask yourself, 'Is all this worth it? Is she worth it?' And most would say she's not."

"Who's *most*?" I asked. "Where are you even getting all this?"

Tony didn't answer me directly. He just told me about Roman Lopez. According to Tony, the Valdez brothers had beat Roman almost to the brink of death. He got it worse than the others because they'd heard that he had been trying to date Lupita without coming to them first. When Roman woke up in the hospital, Lupita was at his side, and she was crying and apologizing for what had happened. She told him that now things would be okay and they could be together. But Roman wouldn't even look at her. He wouldn't even turn in her direction. He never spoke to her again.

"You want to know why?" Tony asked.

I stared at him, unable to answer.

"Because it wasn't fucking worth it," he said. "Maybe he thought it was, but sometimes getting beat senseless is what it takes to knock some sense into you, do you understand what I'm saying?"

My eyes welled with tears again. "Lupita is worth it," I said. "She is."

But Tony wasn't listening. He was shaking his head in disbelief, mumbling, "I can't believe it was you. I really can't. You got some balls, I'll give you that . . ."

"I'm going to fight them," I said, practically blubbering.

"No, you ain't. I guarantee that. And if I was you I'd lay low for a while, let them forget."

CHAPTER FIVE

I

TONY WAS RIGHT, of course. I didn't fight them, and it has been three years now since I last saw Lupita Valdez. So I guess you could say I followed his advice to lay low. I am close to finishing my dissertation; just a few more months of revisions and it will be complete, a worthless, uninspired piece of scholarship, my thesis not even worth mentioning. I didn't follow Professor Kingman's advice—I never found a subject that moved me—but I made it through anyway, as quickly as possible, on sheer momentum. I was already there, I figured, I might as well stay. And that's how three years can pass. I even had a girlfriend, Priscilla, a relationship that lasted over a year and a half. I introduced her to my family, she was friends with my mother, I never had to fight anyone to be with her, never had to prove my love. Which, in the end, wasn't much to prove or fight for. I never stopped thinking about Lupita, not for a day, not even for an hour. She was always in the forefront of my mind; I knew that she was so near, that if I was really bold I could drive to her house, knock on her door, and maybe, maybe she'd answer. Always I thought I saw her. I would see someone with similar hair or a shirt she used to wear, or someone who stood like her, resting on her heel, hip jutting out. I would see her car or a car like hers in the distance, blocks away, and that was enough to make my heart pound. I couldn't help it, no matter how many times I told myself that she couldn't possibly be in a particular place at a particular time of day—at a table studying in the library stacks late at night, for instance—I would still feel nervous, I would still pass by just to make sure. For a while I thought my new relationship would help me recover, but it made it even harder. I kept comparing her to Lupita. On the surface Priscilla made so much more sense for me—she was getting her doctorate in sociology, she had gone to the East Coast for her undergrad, we had long philosophical discussions, we read each other's papers, and she was even half-Mexican, half-white and it was a relief never having to explain what that entailed. But the feelings were never there, no matter how hard I tried to make them exist. Priscilla ended the relationship. She told me that I kept myself at a distance. She kept hoping that would change, but she felt no closer to me than when we first began dating. It was a relief to break up, to no longer feel guilty about where my thoughts wandered or what truly caused my heart to pang.

If I ever had any doubts about my love for Lupita, they disappeared as the years passed and she remained as present in my thoughts and desires as she had for the months we shared together. Every day I imagined I would arrive home and she would be there, even though I eventually moved from that first studio apartment. Somehow, I imagined, she would find me. I would come around the corner, and down the long walkway there she is in front of my door, wearing her work clothes. Her back is toward me, and I slow my pace as I approach. Maybe she is writing something. And my legs feel weak and my heart is pounding. I don't know what to do. After so much time, what do I say? "Lupita," I call out, but it comes out strange, high pitched and hoarse, so I clear my throat and say again, "Lupita." She turns around now, startled. She tries to say something, but she's too flustered. We both are. "Do you want to come in?" I ask. She doesn't answer. She just stares into my eyes, but I'm unable to hold her gaze, not with her staring at me like that, as though she loves me. For so long I could only see her eyes on the day she ended things, her cold, distant look, as if I were a stranger. Those were the eyes burned into my memory, and I can't forgive her for this so quickly, as if she'd done me no harm. But now she is looking at me with different eyes, erasing from my memory that day years before, erasing all the painful days since, the hours of agony spent thinking of my failures, how I didn't fight for her. She holds out the piece of paper in her hand. "I didn't think you'd be home," she says. "I was writing you a note." I take it from her and read it. "I came because I can't live another day without you. Let's run away together," it says. I look up at her, matching her gaze, and I rush toward her and she rushes toward me and we meet with a force neither of us intended, but we hold each other tightly, never wanting to let go again, and she begins to sob, "I'm so sorry, I'm so sorry." And I ask her, "Why did you do that? Why?" And she doesn't hesitate to explain about her brothers finding out; how they were going to kill me; how she had to end it to save me; how she was so cruel that day because otherwise she wouldn't have been able to go through with it. Because she would've given in . . .

Three years of these thoughts, these daydreams, not wanting to have them but having them anyway, as though if I imagined it often enough it would actually come true. But she was never there waiting for me. Even after Priscilla broke up with me, I hoped I would meet someone else to consume my thoughts. But no one compared to Lupita. I finally decided that when I received my degree I would leave Davis, I would leave Woodland. Maybe that's what would finally put her behind me. I needed to move away from everything that reminded me of her. I needed to be far enough away that once and for all I could stop imagining that I would come home to find her at my doorstep.

And maybe that's what would've happened if Mervyn's hadn't gone bankrupt and closed all its stores. When I first learned of it I thought immediately of Lupita. I wondered what she would do now. For weeks I passed by the Yolo County Mall and saw large banners announcing the closeout sales, the discounts growing larger and larger—25 percent off, 40 percent, 60 percent, then 70 percent—until finally I saw a sign that said, "Store Closing Tomorrow—Everything Must Go!" It was evening already, and the store would be closing soon. I was on Gibson Avenue heading toward the freeway to get to Davis, and I decided to pull into the parking lot. I found a space and lingered there for a while without shutting off the engine. I didn't know why I was there. I didn't know what I was going to do. But then suddenly I felt an urge to see the place where Lupita and I had first crossed paths again. I shut off the car and quickly got out before I changed my mind.

I knew the store was going to be empty, but I was unprepared for the utter desolation. It looked like the store had been looted during a riot. Clothes were piled high on racks or strewn about on the floor. The racks and shelves were mostly empty, and some were partially disassembled. Two Mexican men in work clothes and boots struggled to carry a glass display case for jewelry and watches. They walked carefully, sidestepping empty boxes and articles of clothing. Before, I would've known exactly where the shoe section was located, but all the artificial markers were gone. The men's section, the young men's section just across the way, the section with underwear and socks—it was all one large vacuous room now, disorienting me. I followed the linoleum path until I found what remained of the shoe section. The shelves were empty—just a lone rack displaying a few pairs of oversized dress shoes. The display tables were gone, and so was the chair where I once sat with my wet socks, trying on the loafers that I would eventually return. I stood where the chair would've been, and I turned in the direction where Lupita had been standing, and I remembered her beautiful eyes staring at me, and her nervousness. She had actually been unsure whether I would remember her. A feeling of sadness came over me as I stared at the remnants of the Mervyn's shoe section. I thought it strange to attach so much significance to that place, a department store like any other department store, a shoe section like any other shoe section, with all the consumer trappings, but finding it so desolate and sterile was just another reminder that everything was gone; that my love for Lupita was like this place, like a goddamn fucking Mervyn's, as ridiculous as that sounds. It was gigantic and empty. It was over.

And then I saw her. She was less than fifty feet away. She was dressed casually in a T-shirt and jeans, and her long black hair was down. She didn't look like she was working. She was carrying a few shirts in one hand and was perusing a rack of men's clothes. I couldn't move, my feet felt stuck to the ground. My heart was beating fast, and at any moment I expected her to turn my way, but she remained focused on the shirts, slowly pushing a few aside, examining one, pushing it aside, and then examining another. Finally she picked one off the rack, a striped collared shirt, and held it up. "Do you like this?" she called out. I followed the direction of her question. My heart sank when I saw a tall, muscular guy with a shiny bald head. At first I thought it might be one of her brothers, but it wasn't. He wore a tank top, and I could see his arms, chest, and neck covered in tattoos. His face was long and chiseled, and his nose was crooked as if it had been broken several times. He looked like a boxer. I felt weak, and my heart was beating even faster, and I still couldn't move, and a part of me even wanted to break down crying right there, but in a way I also felt relieved. She had moved on. Now I needed to.

I started to walk away when I saw the guy approach Lupita from behind. She was still focused on the shirts on the rack. He towered over her. He placed his bare arms around her, arms that looked like pythons about to strangle her, and he bent down to nuzzle his face into her neck. She shrugged him off, but he didn't let go. Instead he laughed and kissed her cheek so loud that I heard it. She shrugged him off again, her eyes briefly widening in anger. He let go, smiling, and turned away to look at another rack of clothes. Lupita closed her eyes and grimaced. My heart surged. Something told me it wasn't just a momentary annoyance. It was a look of resignation. She was unhappy. She didn't love him. I quickly exited the store, charting my path carefully so that I left unnoticed. I returned to my car shaking with excitement. It was dusk and the parking lot lights flickered on. There was no way that guy understood her as I did. There was no way he fulfilled her as I could. There was no one else for Lupita but me. I was never surer of that fact. I got inside my car and sat there for a while, not able to turn my key in the ignition. I placed my hands on the steering wheel, clenching it. I wanted to cry out her name. I couldn't live my life any longer without her.

"Fuck it!" I yelled, and I actually punched the dashboard three times, one for every year I'd suffered the consequences of my inaction.

II

I cross Beamer and head down Fifth Street. Two little kids pass by on their bikes, staring at me hard. Two old men wearing straw cowboy hats are standing in a walkway, talking. They stop their conversation as I pass. I nod to them in greeting, and they nod in return. "Buen día," they say. I think they look at me strangely. I wonder if it's clear that I'm on my way to a fight. I am walking briskly, I know that, but in my face do I wear the look of someone on his way to his death? Is it fear, is it determination, or is it the face of a man gone insane? Three years since Lupita ended our relationship, and now out of the blue I am returning to do what I should have done then. But I didn't know then what I know now, that for three years I would live with the idea of not fighting them, that her presence would not leave me. Three years of agony, of failure.

I told Tony and he tried to dissuade me. He unleashed the full force of his pessimism. But it wasn't enough. I ignored his comments. I told him that nothing else mattered. If I fought them and she still didn't want to be with me, then fine, then that's how it had to be and I would accept it. But until then I wouldn't ever be able to let it rest. He shook his head and exclaimed, "Three years, man! It's been three years!" And I had his words ringing in my head as I passed Victory Lane, but I knew he could never understand how three years could pass so quickly, one day blurring into the next, so that whether three weeks or three years, it didn't matter. Everything remained the same. But then I think, maybe he could understand. Weren't we all still in the same place? Didn't he tell me the Valdez brothers were still to be found on their front porch every afternoon? Didn't Tony still live at home, still work at the cannery for the season, guaranteed to be home 24/7 during the off-season? He would be home now. I pass his apartment, my old house not far away. I contemplate knocking on his door, but I worry that he will convince me not to fight. Maybe subconsciously that's what I want him to do. I continue on.

I had been taking an indirect route to Lupita's house, but now I cut through an empty lot and end up back on Fifth Street. In the distance I can make out Chucho's '83 Cutlass. It now has tires and is painted gold. Chucho must be close to thirty, I think, if not already in his thirties. Then I wonder, what if only one or two of the brothers are there? Would fighting them not count? What if no one was there? Would I come back another day, repeat this walk? What if the brothers were away and only Lupita was home? Would I announce to her, "I am going to fight them to be with you"? What would she say then? The same thing she said three years ago. "It's just not working out," she had said, but that's not what she meant. I won't give her the chance to say that again. I have to fight them first. We have to meet with the fight behind us, the obstacle cleared. The brothers have to be there, I reassure myself. They will be just as I've imagined: Chucho in the walkway on his cell phone, Eddie and Frankie on the porch, beers in hand. I will tell them, "I am in love with your sister. I will do whatever it takes to be with her." I continue walking, my hands shaking. In the front yard I can see the trunk of the large oak tree and where its roots have lifted the sidewalk. I am breathing heavily, and the Oldsmobile is getting larger.

First I see the top of Chucho's shaved head. It is wrinkled and shaped like a pear. He turns slightly, and I can see the curve of his round cheek. As I approach the fence I see that Eddie is standing in the walkway directly in front of me, carrying a large box of strawberries. I hear Chucho ask, "Yo, where'd you get those?" and Eddie responds, "From that midget Guatemalteco on the corner. Gave 'em to me for ten bucks." I'm on the sidewalk in front of their neighbor's home, but soon I pass the wooden fence and the shrub that conceals Chucho's body. He is to my left now, standing in front of his Oldsmobile wearing a grease-stained T-shirt. Eddie is in the walkway, heading toward the front porch, and I see the side of his body, his fat arm covered in tattoos, his protruding stomach. He is wearing khaki shorts and a white tank top. He is large, but his body looks fat and sloppy. He walks slouched over. I don't see Frankie at first, but then out of the corner of my eye I spot his face just barely peeking over the porch railing. He sits far back on the ratty beige recliner, his feet visible just above the railing. Instantly, I make a calculation. Eddie's back is to me; I can jump on him.

I sprint across the lawn, heading straight toward Eddie. He is completely unaware. My heart is pounding and I can hardly believe what my body is doing. I hear Chucho say, "What the fuh—" and Eddie turns slightly, and I see his brow raised in surprise—now he has heard my approach, sensed it—but as he turns and lifts his arms, the box of strawberries in his hands, my legs suddenly turn to lead and the heavy work boots I wore for the occasion grab the thick, dry Bermuda grass and I find myself falling. Instead of grabbing on to Eddie's back and attempting to knock him over, my head slams against his thigh, my face scrapes against his shorts, and my right shoulder slams against the pavement. I look up and find Eddie's flabby face staring down at me. He is still carrying the box of strawberries, and I half expect him to raise them above his head and slam them down on top of me. For a moment I flinch and hold up my hands to protect myself, but his eyes are more confused than alarmed. His brow is furrowed and he says, "What's the matter with you, man?"

I don't answer. I turn on my back and kick his leg. It doesn't faze him. He still looks confused. I take advantage of his stunned reaction to scramble away. Chucho has rushed over, and Frankie has risen from his recliner and is bounding down the steps. They move toward me, and I'm still on my back and I raise my boots and start to kick at them wildly. My boots graze against their shins, but instead of angering them into attack, they are laughing, and Chucho says, "What the fuck is this?" and Frankie, almost gleeful, yells at me, "Calm down, fool!" But I don't calm down. I continue kicking at them. Lunging forward and kicking, all on my back. My back is burning as it rubs against the grass. I lunge for them again.

Chucho says, "What's he saying?" and Eddie says, "I don't know."

Frankie says, "He's making sound effects!"

Only then do I realize I'm making noises as if I'm in a karate movie. Now I cry out, "Fight me! Fight me!"

"What?" Chucho yells back. He is laughing hysterically.

"Grab his leg!" Frankie cries, and both he and Eddie grab hold of my boots, and I struggle to wiggle free. I manage to free myself several times, kicking their hands and forearms. I momentarily back away, and they use the opportunity to charge me, both Frankie and Eddie lunging for my shoulders. I don't know how, but I manage to elbow Eddie in the nose. He pulls away, grabbing it, crying out, "Aw, shit!" In frustration he kicks me hard in the thigh. I barely feel it, but I see that there is blood on his hand. He looks at it for a moment, touches below his nose to find more blood on his fingers, and instantly his face turns red with anger. It is a relief to know that I've wounded him, but my victory is short lived. All of Frankie's limbs are on top of me at once—his arms over my neck and shoulder, his knees digging into my stomach and crotch. I can feel his sweat, the hair on his arms. I can smell his beer breath. Soon both Chucho's and Eddie's faces appear, and they are on top of me too, Eddie's mouth smeared in blood. Chucho holds my left arm, Frankie is on my right, and Eddie is holding down my legs. I struggle to move but I can't so much as squirm. "Fight me!" I cry out, gasping for air. I realize that Chucho's hand is over my neck. He's not choking me but merely preventing me from raising my head. "Quit moving, you little fucking white boy," I hear one of them say.

"Fight me," I cry out again. And this time I collapse backward, my head striking the ground. I can see the blue sky, the leaves of a fig tree, a paint-chipped fence. My body relaxes and I feel the grip on my neck ease.

"What the hell's wrong with you, man?" I hear Eddie say. He is laughing. Now the other two brothers are laughing too. They're laughing at me, but I don't care.

"I'm in love with Lupita," I say. "I'll do whatever it takes to be with her."

This makes them laugh even harder. They still don't let go of me, but their faces are gleeful—even Eddie with the bloody nose. They are smiling from ear to ear as if I've made their day.

"That's why you came to fight us?" Frankie asked, cackling. "So you can be with her, huh?"

"Yes," I say.

"Fool, Lupita don't want to be with your ass," Chucho says to me. "Fucking stupid. It don't work like that. She got a man anyway."

"You think she wants to be with you?" Frankie asks. He reaches for my cheek and pinches it. "Stupid white boy."

"She doesn't love him," I say. "She loves me. We've already been together."

"What the fuck you talking about?" Chucho asks.

"We've already been together. She loves me, I love her. Remember a few years ago when you found out she was dating someone behind your back? That was me! Now I'm here to fight you so we don't have to hide it."

Chucho's face grows dark. He doesn't believe me, but he's also not sure. The situation is too strange for him. I don't take my eyes off his. I can feel Frankie and Eddie's grip on my legs and shoulder tighten.

"You think you're funny, fool?" Eddie says.

"Faggot thinks he's funny," Frankie follows.

Chucho is staring hard into my eyes. He's trying to read me, to see if I'm just crazy.

"You say she loves you," he says.

"Yes."

"Well, let's ask her then. But how about this? She does love you"—he smiles—"and we let you go. We consider your little kicking fit our fight. If she doesn't know you, we're going to beat the living shit out of you. You wanna know why? Because you bloodied Eddie's nose and you made Frankie drop all his damn strawberries. And he loves strawberries. That's why, okay?" Then he turns and cries out Lupita's name. He yells it several times, but she doesn't come out.

"Go get her, Eddie," Chucho says, and then he warns me not

96

to move or he'll punch the shit out of me. I can tell he is angry now, but he is anxious too. He knows something is not right. Eddie lets go of my shoulder and rises to his feet, but before he reaches the steps the screen door creaks open. I can't see Lupita as Chucho blocks my vision, but soon he moves off of me and I can breathe again.

"This white boy say he been with you. That you love each other," Frankie says, cackling.

Lupita's face is lost in the porch's afternoon shadow, but now she moves into the light, squinting her eyes as she walks down the steps. She's scowling. I wait for her to recognize me, but she looks just as she did the day she said good-bye. Cold, distant, a stranger. She stops in the walkway and shields her eyes from the sun. I can't see her eyes, but she scrunches up her face and I know what she's about to say. I don't even have to hear it.

"I don't know him," she says.

The brothers are on me before I can cry out to her or run away or collapse into a ball and hope that I emerge alive. Chucho punches me in the jaw and I feel it dislodge and my teeth feel like they're in the wrong place, like I'm biting down on my molars. I fall to the ground and immediately I try to rise up, but there's a blow to my side and now I can no longer breathe and my head is throbbing and I'm tasting blood and I can't hear a damn thing. It flashes across my mind that I'm about to die, and suddenly nothing matters anymore, because I'm about to die, and I don't care, I just want to die. I try to breathe but it's as if I've forgotten how. The air is there but I have no access to it, there is no way to inhale. But then for no reason my breath returns and my lungs fill with air and not only can I breathe but I can hear again too. I can hear, and at first it's just the sound of my gasps, and I hear the grunts of the Valdez brothers and the dull thuds of their fists hitting my back and side and legs, but then through it all I hear something familiar, and at first I think it is just the ringing in my head, but then it becomes more distinct. I can hear it now. It is Lupita and she is crying out my name.

A Brief Explanation

—∿∿—

for Bradley Bazzle

FIVE YEARS AGO, I accepted a faculty position in the American Studies Department at Grosely College in New Hampshire. I was hired to teach courses in Mexican American History, 1848–1960; Chicano History, 1960–Present; and a primer course on Latinos in America. My classes were poorly attended. It's possible that my reputation as a rigorous professor and grader, especially by the standards of my department, kept students at bay. In addition to weekly quizzes, a midterm, a final, and a final research paper (twenty pages), I assigned four medium-length papers (eight to ten pages), and I rarely gave above a B+. My expectations were high. My student evaluations were usually pretty poor. A correlation? Perhaps, but the students never mentioned this in their reasoning. Instead, they focused on my lecture style, which they disparaged either as "sleep inducing," "condescending," "utterly incomprehensible," or having "no consideration for an audience whatsoever," to list just a few. I tried to make alterations, but the response remained, stubbornly, the same.

Unfortunately, my seminar courses, though intended to be smaller, have been even less well received (thankfully Grosely College prides itself on its teacher-to-student ratio). Two years ago, in my seminar An Exploration of Mexican American Demographic Shifts and Their Impact, 1848–2000, I had only one student register. As a result, the class was relegated to an independent study. But the student dropped after the third week without notifying me. I showed up two weeks in a row before finally e-mailing him to ask his whereabouts. After this, it was suggested by the department chair that I teach a seminar course with a slightly more "entertaining" topic (his exact word).

"Entertaining?" I asked him.

"Yes," he said.

"Entertaining?" I asked again.

"Exactly," he said.

I had no idea what he meant, and he didn't elaborate, but the next week I found a book in my department mailbox entitled *El Gran Juego: Latino Baseball Players in the Major Leagues*. I can only assume it was a hint as to the meaning of entertaining. I e-mailed a Latino colleague of mine in Connecticut and asked about enrollment in his classes. He told me he had no problem filling his seminars. In fact, his most popular seminar was expanded into a lecture course. He claimed to fill a two-hundred-seat auditorium! The class was on Latino gangs. Of course, I had little background on the topic, but when my department chair asked me several weeks later at a staff party whether I had considered any potential subjects for my seminar, I surprised myself by mentioning Latino gangs (it may have been a segue), and I was further surprised when the department chair clasped his hands in excitement and said, "Now that's a class I would be interested in taking!" Then he promptly called over a colleague and informed him that I was to teach my next seminar on Latino gangs. The colleague, a real stickler, asked me what my scholarship on the subject was like—an impertinent question because plenty of professors are required to wing lectures and seminars on subjects far from their subject of expertise. I could have admitted this, said something like, "This will be an exploration endeavored by student and professor alike." But I didn't. Instead, feeling my back against the wall, all eyes on me (because by that time several other colleagues had joined the discussion; the department chair was so enthusiastic about my decision that he was practically waving people over), I said that I had spent time researching the development of Norteño and Sureño gang paraphernalia in San Quentin State Prison. Of course, I hadn't, and all that I knew about San Quentin—and Latino gangs for that matter—came from *Blood In, Blood Out*, a movie I'd last watched when I was sixteen.

Well, I went back to the source. I placed *Blood In, Blood Out* (1993) in my Netflix queue, and then I received several other suggestions based on my interest. *American Me* (1992), starring Edward James Olmos, seemed the most relevant, but I requested them all, watched them, took scrupulous notes, and then ordered several books online (our library had very little available), including an excellent anthology of pinto (or prison) poetry. I asked my colleague in Connecticut for a recommended reading list, which he willingly supplied. Finally, I felt prepared. I wrote up a syllabus, requested books to be stocked in the campus bookstore, and put together a course reader, which, though not as large as my others, was not slim either. When I checked my roster online, I was pleasantly surprised to find my first waiting list! Twenty students were enrolled, with fifteen waiting expectantly behind them. My department chair congratulated me over e-mail and even included an exuberant postscript: "Add me to next semester's roster!"

The class went well; the students seemed genuinely interested, and I didn't hear one complaint about the course requirements (though I did reduce the number of essays). The discussion was always very lively. As I became more comfortable with the subject matter, I found myself personalizing some of my contributions, which is something I did frequently in my other courses. As a Chicano, or a Latino, I've long felt that my personal anecdotes not only enrich the conversation but also promote students' understanding that Chicano and Latino history are a fundamental part of American society. I see myself, then, as a key representative of this idea. For many students,

I'm the only Latino instructor they've ever had and maybe one of the few Latinos they'll meet in their four years at Grosely. In other words, I better make it count. With this in mind, I don't always insist on strict accuracy when it comes to my personal anecdotes. For example, my own father growing up in Los Angeles in the 1940s remembers watching three drunken sailors beat up his older brother. Why not mention this anecdote in a discussion pertaining to the infamous Zoot Suit Riots of 1943? Never mind that two of the sailors were our cousins, and my uncle was a notorious provoker; nor does it matter that it was Christmas of 1949. In the end, the point is this: tensions between sailors and Mexican American youth ran high for many years.

Well, in the seminar I found myself talking more and more about my own memories of gang culture during my junior high and high school years. Of course, I never participated in the least, but I was aware of its existence, and I do believe I made this clear to my students. Nevertheless, perhaps owing to my growing excitement in the subject and the ease with which I was able to relate it to my own life, the students received the impression that my high school was teeming with hardened criminals and that I had barely escaped a life of violence myself. I can't say that I did much to dispel this impression once I became aware of it. In truth, I had always wished to be more than a good student or an educator like both my parents, and though my path had always been relatively clear—smooth sailing, really—I didn't mind imagining it as somehow riddled with obstacles. That was my initial mistake: I didn't discourage the students' view that they were in the presence of someone with not only scholarly authority but also "street" authority, or "cred" as it's called.

I taught the same seminar the following semester, once again with a long waiting list. Except now, rather than students *gaining* the impression that I knew firsthand about Latino gang life, they entered class—having talked, I'm sure, to the previous semester's students—with the idea that I was something of a reformed gangster, having "made it out" or "lived to tell it how it was"; one success story among thousands of failures. Even our department chair approached me one afternoon, placed his hand on my shoulder, and said, "I had no idea, I really had no idea." I can only assume what he was referring to. It didn't help matters either that on my wife's request I had decided to grow a goatee and shave my head, a final remedy to my steady hair loss over the past two years. She thinks I resemble Victorio Zuburán, the Mexican anarchist, and she has always encouraged the resemblance. My students, of course, had no idea who Victorio Zuburán was or what he looked like, and my poor attempt at an intellectual's facial hair circa 1910 only furthered their impression that their professor was the real deal; apparently I looked like a man not to be messed with. It was remarked upon, after viewing the independent film, *Living the Loco Life* (1987), which we did in the second week, that I resembled Chucho, one of the principal characters; also a murderer.

This brings me to the two students directly pertaining to my case. Karen Ribold, a junior American Studies major, and Rodrigo Gabiria, a sophomore, major undeclared. Karen was a model student: inquisitive, engaging, and a clear writer. She was also very attractive; one could almost say captivating. I had heard her name mentioned before by students and professors alike, and not in regard to her intellectual faculties. Rodrigo Gabiria, a Colombian, was one of the few Latinos on campus. He grew up in Washington, DC. I don't know why he chose Grosely College, though I heard he was recruited for our basketball team but injured himself early on. At first, Rodrigo was not a model student: he rarely participated in class discussions, he never came to office hours, and usually by the end of our two-hour class he would rest his head on the table and appear to sleep. His writing style, however, was superb, eloquent even. He was also something of a ladies' man, always complimenting the female students in class—decent things, such as that he appreciated their take on a passage in our reading, or something equally benign, but he never spoke to the male students in this way. With them he usually joked around, engaged in the usual male banter. They all liked him. In fact, everyone liked him. He had a magnetic quality that I can't deny him. For his part, he seemed to have his eyes on Karen Ribold. Unfortunately for him, she had her eyes on me.

I didn't encourage it, but I was certainly flattered by her attention. At first I assumed it was purely academic, but soon I realized that it was more ardent—probably after she visited my office hours for the fifth time, having no questions, merely requesting somewhat vaguely "if I could elaborate further on what was discussed in class that day." I did elaborate, and I soon found that she was most curious to hear my own anecdotes about gang life. Of course, I wasn't talking from my own experience directly, but it seemed that for every example I gave she would follow with, "And so, what was it like for you, you know, growing up in those conditions?" I did my best to explain that "the conditions" weren't exactly personally experienced by me but were more accurately witnessed from afar, but it was almost as if she didn't want to believe me, or that she thought I was acting bashful or humble, not wishing to overstate my predicament. Whenever she asked about my childhood she would refer to it as "your life in the barrio." I explained—pretty clearly, I thought—that I grew up a few streets *over* from an apartment complex that could be considered barrio-esque, but I guess I can be faulted for not revealing that I inhabited a nineteenth-century Victorian described by the town's Stroll-through-History Committee as a "colorful gem not to me missed." If I was more aware of these kinds of things (Karen's feelings, that is), I could've put a stop to them early on, but I am notoriously obtuse when it comes to the attentions of the opposite sex. Just ask my wife; even after our ninth date I still thought she was curious to know more about my dissertation on Article V of the Treaty of Guadalupe Hidalgo. Anyhow, that was my second mistake: I didn't do enough to distance myself from Karen Ribold.

As I mentioned, Rodrigo Gabiria was interested in Karen and must have resented the attention she gave me. Soon he went on the offensive. At first I didn't notice the pointed nature of his comments. I just assumed that, as the other Latino in the class, he had a right to add to my personal anecdotes with stories of his own—the morals of which, I should mention, often conflicted with mine. For instance, and this is the example that sticks clearest in my mind, I often emphasized that young Latino males turn to gang life because they lack sufficient alternatives—they are underserved by their schools and community programs—but Rodrigo argued the opposite. In his school, a private Catholic school in DC, they had plenty of activities, such as sports, student government, art classes, and Latino Club. Nevertheless, many of his friends turned to what he continually referred to as "thug life," because it was simply "much, much cooler" than anything else. "Even speaking for myself," he said, "basketball star, starting quarterback, junior-class president, even I participated in certain activities that may or may not be considered legal." When he said this, he cocked his head in my direction and looked at me accusingly, narrowing his gaze, as though wanting me to know that he hadn't said it for the sake of class discussion, but for my sake and my sake only (and perhaps for Karen Ribold). At the time, I had no idea why he did this; I just noted the fact. The comment created a stir, and the students clamored to know more about his checkered past. Smugly, he said that he didn't want to incriminate himself. "But basically," he said, "my point is this: everyone wants respect, everyone wants to be tough, not to mention the fact that every young Latino male wants to attract young females, and therein lies one's motivation." Then he added, clearly feigning remorse, "I did things I'm not proud of, but I can't see it being any different." You should have heard the class! And you should have watched him hold court for the rest of the session.

I wouldn't have cared, really. I was happy that Rodrigo felt comfortable talking about his experiences, and it didn't matter that his experiences conflicted with mine, or at least with the perspective I'd gathered from the texts recommended by my colleague in Connecticut. Contradictions were important for discussion and debate. But it soon became clear, to me, at least, that it wasn't just his aim to bring attention to himself;

he wanted to prove to the class, and to Karen Ribold in particular, that I was a liar. More specifically, that I had invented stories about my own participation in the so-called thug life. For instance, I didn't remember claiming to have walked around my hometown with a red bandana on my head, but I did say something to that effect. In truth, I had walked around once, around my house, in a bandana that was more maroon than red, because I thought it would relax my increasingly wavy and unruly hair (it didn't, much to my dismay, but how I wish I had that full head of hair today!). Of course, I didn't mention these details in class, but I figured that if pressed I could easily excuse myself based on semantics. So I thought. Several classes later, Rodrigo decided to challenge me on the red-bandana claim. He said, "If you really walked around town wearing a red bandana you must've had to fight some fool every other block." I responded that I never *exactly* said that I wore the red bandana *around* town, and that was when Karen interrupted and said that two class sessions before I had indeed indicated that I had. She pointed to her notes: "Professor looks down at his hands, grimaces, looks up at the class, his eyes staring off as if into the past, and says, 'I wasn't afraid to walk around my hometown flaunting the color red on my head. That's just what one had to do . . .'" Apparently, I had said it. I saved myself by saying that I knew which blocks to walk and which ones not to. Karen Ribold smiled approvingly. Rodrigo Gabiria smirked.

It continued this way for several class sessions. I ceased interjecting in the discussions, except to refer directly to the class reading. I was more guarded now, but Rodrigo always found a way to remind the class of some story I had previously shared. On a discussion about the links between Los Angeles youth street gangs and Mexican drug cartels, the name El Caballo Sanchez of Juliacán was mentioned for a second time, and it would've been quickly forgotten if not for Rodrigo reminding the class that I had claimed (the first time around) to know the nephew of El Caballo Sanchez. The truth is, I did know the nephew of a *certain* El Caballo Sanchez, an old man who lived on my aunt's street in Bakersfield, and when I'd first come across the name I jumped at the opportunity to mention it, quickly realizing they were not one and the same. El Caballo Sanchez of Bakersfield was a security guard at the flea market, not the violent head of a drug cartel. But it was too late. The claim was made, recorded in Karen Ribold's notebook for posterity, and of course also in Rodrigo Gabiria's memory, tucked away for later use. So I was forced to admit to the class that I had been mistaken. They didn't really seem to care. Karen, on the other hand, appeared confused, Rodrigo properly smug.

By then I had surmised what was going on, and I wasn't going to let it go any farther. Following class one day, I asked Rodrigo to visit me in my office hours, and instead of readily agreeing like any other student, he asked, "What for?" I told him I was interested to hear more about his high school experiences and the possibility of including them in his final paper. "Well, can't we just talk about it now?" he asked uncouthly. It was after class and there were still students milling about. I told him to walk with me back to the department. He accepted this, and as soon as we were alone I said to him, "Look, Rodrigo, it seems like you have something against me. Like you wish to prove something, and I don't understand why. Or maybe I do understand, but I want to tell you that you don't need to do it. There's enough room for two of our perspectives. We shouldn't be trying to undermine one another, but rather supporting our individual endeavors. After all, there are so few of us out here." And he responded, "I'm not trying to undermine you. In fact, it seems to me that you undermine yourself every time you talk. This don't have anything to do with us both being Latino. As far as I'm concerned, you're a phony, a fake."

"And just what am I faking, Rodrigo?" I asked.

"You know exactly what you're faking, but if you want me to say it—"

I interrupted him and said, "If you're going to accuse me of falsehood, you might as well accuse yourself of the same. We're both children of certain privilege, allowed entrance, if you will, into the ivory tower, and yet your macho posturing is no different than—"

Now he interrupted me. "Macho posturing? Is that what it's called in your sociology texts? Well, I'll tell you what. My dad abandoned me and my mom when I was two. My mom cleans hotel rooms. I got to Bishop Prep on a scholarship, but when most kids got picked up in their Range Rovers to go back to the suburbs after school, I walked home with my other scholarship friends through the fucking—"

Now I interrupted him and said that clearly he was angry and that if we were to discuss this any further he would have to change the tone of his voice. He simply told me that he didn't have time for this and walked off. It struck me as strange that Rodrigo would end the conversation in this way, not to mention conduct himself so insolently toward me in general, with no worry whatsoever that the man he was insulting was the very one with the power to pass or fail him. But then I remembered his eloquent writing style and the quality of his written assignments in class thus far. I realized he had great confidence in his abilities and knew that if he was given a grade he didn't approve of he could easily appeal it based on his work. Not to mention the fact that he had started participating more in class discussion, albeit at my expense. I knew I had no leverage over him.

The day before I was to travel home for Thanksgiving break, Karen Ribold showed up at my office. It wasn't during office hours, which I usually stick to, but she had a look of urgent distress, and I wasn't about to turn her away. I asked her to have a seat and rose to open the door, which she had closed (I kept the door open with all of my students; you can never be too safe). I asked her what was wrong, and immediately she burst into tears. Thinking to comfort her, I instinctively put out my hand to pat her shoulder, but then I thought better of it and pulled back. I wished to avoid any confusion or mixed signals. "Now, now, Karen," I said, "tell me what it is. You've done an excellent job so far in class." She looked up, her eyes red, her face almost expressing physical pain. "Is it true that you've made everything up?" she cried. "Is it true that both your parents are high school administrators? That you know nothing of the barrio, of gang life? That you've based your experience on pure hearsay? That you've—"

She would have continued, but I had to stop her. She was practically hyperventilating. Until that moment I didn't comprehend the depth of her feelings for me. I merely assumed it was some harmless schoolgirl crush. I now recognized the expression on her face. It was that of a betrayed lover. It's unwise for a professor to involve himself in the affairs of his students, but in this case, as it directly involved me, I decided to intervene.

"Let me guess," I said. "You've been talking to Rodrigo."

She nodded her head as she found a tissue and wiped her nose. "How did you know?" she asked.

"Well, it seems he has some sort of vendetta against me," I said, "and wishes to prove that I'm less of a man than he is. I don't know why, but he's made it his mission to prove that he's more macho than I am or something. But I have nothing to prove. It must stem from some insecurity of his. I'm sure he feels very alone here in New Hampshire, far from his gente, his familia, his cultura. I know how he feels."

She seemed to appreciate this. "So it's not true then? You didn't make anything up?"

"No, not at all," I said, choosing my words carefully. "I mean, I did have a more privileged upbringing than many of my friends, but we certainly observed many of the same experiences." Then I told her that I had to finish wrapping up my work because I was flying back to California that evening.

"Will you see your friends?" she asked—somewhat randomly, I thought.

"Yeah, sure, I assume so."

She suddenly grew animated. "You know what would be really cool? If you were able to bring one of your friends as like a guest speaker or something. In other classes they always bring in some boring academic, but in this case it'd be awesome to meet an actual expert, you know."

I told her it sounded like a fabulous idea, but I did so more to cheer her up than anything else. For one, I didn't plan on seeing any friends from back home. I didn't really forge strong bonds until college, and most of those friends were scattered around the country. The only high school friend I kept in touch with was Manny Solis, and when I considered the countless lunch-time hours spent doing homework (usually others' for a small profit), I didn't think our illicit activity was what Karen had in mind. She wiped her eyes, thanked me for my time, and told me she had read one of my books. I thanked her and said the perfunctory, "So *you're* the one!" We laughed. An awkward silence followed. I think she wanted to hug me good-bye, but again I refrained from any physical contact. I saw her to the door and hoped that I had seen the worst of this strange triangle.

But as luck would have it, on my first day back home I was running an errand for my mother and I saw a vaguely familiar face in the produce section. My hometown isn't that large, so I'd seen plenty of familiar faces over the years, but I'd long ceased reacting to them as if they were on the verge of recognizing me. I blame it on my weight gain and hair loss; or maybe I'm just better at remembering faces than the average person. Well, this familiar face was wide and dark skinned. He had a shaved head and a trimmed goatee. He was large, six foot two at least, and as broad as the shopping cart he pushed in front of him. I looked away, not wanting to make eye contact, but he must've had no such qualms, because suddenly I heard, "Hey, brother, brother, I remember you from high school!" I smiled at him, still not able to place his face, and I extended my hand in greeting, which he pushed aside in order to give me a bear hug. "Brother, brother!" he kept saying as he held me. With his arms around me, my face practically smothered by his massive chest, I finally realized who the man was. It was Payaso (the Clown) Garza, one of the most feared Sureños in my entire school. We had had a class together our junior year, health or some other required course where everyone was thrown together. We sat next to each other; in fact, on several occasions I had assisted him with an answer or two.

"Payaso," I said, "it's great to see you."

"No, brother, call me Frank. I gave up banging years ago. Those were dark, dark times, but after many prayers the Lord helped me find my way to the light."

"That's great," I said.

"Brother, where you at now?"

"I'm a professor. In New Hampshire."

"What?!" he exclaimed, a huge smile coming over his face. "That's wonderful, brother, that's so good to hear. Bless Jesus!"

"Yes, for sure," I said.

I proceeded to tell him I'd published a few books, and he swore to me that he was going to find them at the bookstore. I told him he'd probably have better luck online. We spoke for ten minutes, maybe even more, he asking most of the questions and responding to each of my answers with praises for Jesus. He never stopped smiling. I had the feeling that running into me had made his day. I was flattered. We were about to part ways when Karen Ribold's request popped into my head, and I thought, "Here is the perfect guest speaker!" I immediately pitched him the opportunity. I would fly him out to Grosely College and have him talk about his experiences in gang life and how he ultimately left it behind. He was reluctant at first, but when I told him that the students would benefit enormously from his message, he agreed. I also made clear that all of his expenses would be covered. He told me he had never been to the East Coast before. So it was decided, and for the next few days I felt a sense of relief. I guess I hadn't realized how much Rodrigo's accusations had bothered me. I didn't deserve to be called a phony, to be accused of inventing falsehoods. My aim was to enrich my students' education, that was it, and I had my ways of achieving this; others had their own methods, but my fundamental goal was opening minds, and I didn't deserve to be treated like a fraud. Though my friendship with Frank Garza, so far as I knew, could only be based on the times I allowed him to copy my homework and a few tests, somehow my reunion with a feared Sureño gangster vindicated me. I *had* spoken from my own experience. The Payaso Garzas of the world were a part of me, and the Rodrigo Gabirias had no right to take that away. I knew I shouldn't have allowed myself to continue in this vein, but the honest truth is that I looked forward to seeing Rodrigo's face when I introduced our honored guest.

But soon my excitement waned. The more I thought about it, or the more I thought about Frank Garza, the more I started to analyze the nature of our brief interaction. In retrospect, he almost seemed goofy. It wasn't just the incessant referencing of Jesus, or calling me brother over and over, or the bear hug he gave me upon greeting and parting; there was, for lack of a better word, a cheesy quality about him. As if in exchange for his soul he had given up his manhood. Though his physical presence was to be contended with, his demeanor was almost laughable. Only a simpleton could be so happy-go-lucky. It was as if he had finally become the clown his gangster nickname professed him to be. The Payaso Garza I remembered was a man among boys. He walked into a room and everyone quieted. He spoke to you and you trembled. He asked to look at your test and you gave it to him. Payaso Garza, for all his faults, and for all the trouble he probably caused his parents and school administrators, was someone who commanded respect. Frank Garza, on the other hand, wasn't.

I proceeded anyway, my impression of Frank deepening with each successive phone call to hammer out logistics, confirm dates, etc. I started to imagine that my plan to bring him (and allay Rodrigo's attacks) would backfire. I imagined that the class would be disappointed. "*This* was one of the most feared Sureños in your hometown?" they would say. They wanted to see the wise strong man, Smiley, from *The Homies* (1992), or the repentant but stoic Luis Rodriguez from the classic memoir *Always Running*, or even the hardened lyrical voice of prison poets like Raúl Salinas. Instead, I bring them a fundamentalist teddy bear. With this in mind, and on what I can only describe as a desperate whim, I thumbed through the phone book, and to my surprise I came across the name Eziquel Marquez, also known as Easy, probably the most feared gangster in the entire city. Even more feared than

112

Payaso Garza. He had been expelled from school my senior year for smashing a kid's face against the pavement and then fighting off four school cops who made the mistake of tasing him. Prior to that incident, I had also assisted him with a test or two. I wondered if he would remember me.

I hesitated before dialing the number, asking myself whether I was doing this for the sake of my class's educational enrichment or if it was just to prove to Rodrigo Gabiria and Karen Ribold that I hadn't misrepresented myself. Before answering that question to any satisfaction, I found myself dialing, I heard myself talking to Eziquel Marquez Sr., I heard him pass the phone to Eziquel Marquez Jr., who, it was explained to me, just happened to be at his parents' home. I heard myself telling him who I was, what I was interested in, and asking if he would be willing to travel to New Hampshire. All I remember him saying was, "How much?" I told him $300 plus expenses, the standard honorarium. He countered with $750, and I heard myself agree. Then he said, very matter-of-factly, "Call me Easy, not Eziquel." I stuttered out an apology and said that of course I remembered his nickname, and I was about to tell him about Payaso Garza reverting back to Frank, but then I thought otherwise, or he hung up on me, I don't remember.

There were only two class sessions before reading week, and then finals. As it happened, both Frank and Easy could make it on the same day. I didn't think this would be a problem. In fact, I thought it might be preferable to present the two case studies simultaneously. By this time I had resolved in my mind that I had invited the two former gang members as an important way for the students to learn about this particular experience. It wasn't enough to just read about it—gangs as some abstract phenomena—one must actually meet people whose lives were affected by the activity. I felt myself in a privileged position to offer my students this opportunity, and I even decided to extend an invitation to my colleague in Connecticut, who, though impressed with the idea, was not able to attend, and to the department chair, who said he "wouldn't miss it for the world."

Frank Garza flew in the evening before class and spent the night at my place. I had offered him a hotel, but he told me a couch was fine, and after spending an additional $450 of my department allotment on Easy's honorarium, I wasn't about to insist otherwise. My wife liked to entertain guests, but unfortunately she was out of town for work. Still, she left out sheets, a towel, and a note that said, "Hope to meet you someday, Frank!" He seemed very touched by the gesture. Easy was to fly in the morning of class, which worried me because of the season and weather delays, but there was nothing I could do about it. I instructed him to take a cab directly to campus, and I'd have a student lead him to the classroom. The evening and morning with Frank Garza were insufferable. The man never shut up, he never stopped smiling, and he never ceased praising Jesus. I didn't tell him I was an atheist, and by the time we'd prayed three times—hands locked, eyes closed—I figured it was too late.

We left for class early because Frank wanted to see a little of the campus, but as we walked across Grosely's central quad I could see that he had grown nervous. I told him not to worry, that the students would be interested in anything he had to say. I still hadn't heard from Easy, and I was beginning to worry, but really, so worn down by my time with Frank Garza, I just wanted to get through class, bring him to the airport, and have it all be over. The department chair was waiting inside the classroom along with the other students. He told me he'd watch from a chair in the corner, but I insisted he join us around the table. The class started with still no word from Easy. I proceeded anyway. I introduced Frank, formerly known as Payaso, and gave a few memories that I had of him from high school. Before turning it over to him, I acknowledged that we were friends, but Frank corrected me. "Brothers," he said. "We're brothers," which, to be honest, made me flush with pride. I couldn't help but look at Karen Ribold, who was smiling just as proudly, and at Rodrigo Gabiria, who was sizing up Frank as if he were about to challenge him to a fight.

Then Frank began talking, not about gangs, but about Jesus

Christ and how he had allowed Him to enter into his heart. This went on for about ten minutes. Repeatedly, I tried interrupting, asking questions specifically related to his involvement with the infamous Sureño gang, but he knew what he was doing. He didn't want to talk about gangs, not specifically anyway; he wanted to talk about the devil and temptation and false pride, he wanted to talk about poverty of spirit, about redemption. The students were confused. A few of them raised their hands to ask questions, but Frank ignored them, and soon they lowered their hands. Then they lost interest. Several times I noticed the department chair checking his watch. So it was a relief when I finally received the text message from Easy Marquez, notifying me that he was on campus. Without hesitating, I interrupted Frank and asked the class if anybody would volunteer to bring our other guest speaker to the classroom. Only Rodrigo Gabiria offered, rising from his seat before I could think of an alternative. I told him he was waiting by the campus gates. "There's another speaker?" Frank asked disappointedly. "Yes," I said, feeling little sympathy for him at the moment, "He will be speaking about *gangs* as well."

Frank continued, and, as though he had caught my drift, he lessened his spiel on Jesus and shifted his focus to how he had first been initiated into the 5th Street Locos at the age of eleven, how he used to be a lookout for his father and uncles as they dealt drugs, and how on his thirteenth birthday he watched his uncle die from a stab wound. The class was captivated now. They hung on to his every word, and even the department chair sat forward in his seat. I, too, was engrossed in Frank's story. So engrossed, in fact, that I didn't notice when Rodrigo Gabiria and Easy Marquez entered the room. I only noticed when Frank stopped talking and the goofy pleased-with-the-world smile disappeared from his face. He looked like the wind had been knocked out of him. "What's the meaning of this, brother?" he asked, his jovial tone gone.

The entire class turned to see who had entered. I hadn't seen Easy in more than fifteen years, and whereas time had softened Frank, it had clearly hardened his counterpart. I had never seen anyone look so utterly and completely mean. That was it, no other way to describe it: just mean. He also arrived wearing a red baseball hat, an oversized red parka, perfectly pressed khakis, and red tennis shoes. Then I remembered: he was a Norteño. No, he *is* a Norteño. Why hadn't I considered that? Rodrigo sat down, a smirk on his face, as if he knew something that no one else did. I wondered what the two had talked about on the way over. Easy sat down too, not once taking his eyes off of Frank. I looked over at Frank and asked him to continue his story, but Frank's face had hardened as well. It was as if he had two masks: a soft-faced friendly one, the proselytizing teddy bear, and then this one, with a stare as hardened and cold as Easy's. At that point, I realized I had made a horrible, horrible mistake. Why didn't I think it would be an atrocious idea to invite two former gang members to the same guest lecture? Why didn't I think to remember their separate affiliations? I guess the key word here is "former." I had assumed that both were reformed. Easy most definitely was not. Frank certainly was, but it was now obvious to the entire room as he clutched the seminar table so hard that the veins in his hands and forearms popped out: Frank Garza was in turmoil, fighting his inner demons, struggling to contain the dark forces of the devil he had so exuberantly described earlier. Unbeknown to me at the time (but I learned later), years ago, around the time Frank was attempting to leave gang life behind, Easy, in a deliberate act of provocation, had behaved inappropriately toward Frank's younger sister. He may have given her a black eye. Some say it was much worse. Frank had prayed for the strength to forgive, and after much prayer he had found that strength. Now he was face-to-face with the man, and in New Hampshire of all places, at Grosely College, in my classroom. This test of his strength was apparently too much to endure. Especially when Easy said, "How's Mayra, Scrap?" "Scrap" is what Norteños call Sureños.

I don't remember exactly what happened after that. There was a fight, I know, and I was knocked unconscious in the melee. I was happy to learn (much to my surprise) that I had attempted to get in between the two men, albeit unsuccessfully.

116

But I couldn't prevent what had been brewing for years. The campus police were called, and thanks to the intervention of the department chair both men were released. I can only assume they made it home okay. The students held an impromptu discussion following the fight, which I heard lasted several hours. The department chair was privy to part of the conversation and later told me he was impressed with my students' level of involvement with the subject matter. Despite the horrifying violence, it was certainly an educational experience. I agreed with him, and I assumed that would be the last of it.

I thought no more of the incident until I received the final research papers and read through Rodrigo Gabiria's. It was a beautifully written account, beginning with the fight between Frank and Easy and then tracing back through all that I had done to falsely represent myself as a "gang member" or as someone with "raw knowledge" of gang life. Using Karen Ribold's extensive notes, everything I'd ever said in class had been vetted for accuracy. He had even called my parents, telling them he was writing a bio piece on me, and asked them about my upbringing. He portrayed me as a buffoon, as a liar, as someone who would invent any falsehood if it meant ingratiating myself with gullible Anglo students thirsting for knowledge about Latinos, not to mention my female students, whom I was particularly fond of seducing with my wild anecdotes. He wrote that I even went so far as to pay off a known gang member and violent criminal to say we were friends. His intent, other than lampooning me, was to sort through the schizophrenic effects of a post-ethnic and post-racial academic culture on those subscribing to old-school definitions of identity politics. I read the paper calmly, removed, knowing it was a malicious attack on my character but also agreeing with much of its premise. I just couldn't believe that *I* was the case in point. Though I was tempted to write a long letter justifying my actions, by then I was so tired of the ordeal, of the menace of Rodrigo Gabiria in particular, that I just wanted to be done with it. I wrote him an e-mail telling him that I received his final essay and that, though very nicely written, it was not a research paper. At best it was a political tract, at worst an opinion piece. I would give him an extra week to hand in a separate essay conforming to the class requirements. But he ignored my request. He wrote back a week later, snidely thanking me for my compliments and informing me that I wasn't alone in my high estimation of his prose. A campus journal had just notified him that they were considering his essay for publication.

I found this amusing. I thought he meant the student-run newspaper, the *Grosely Gazette*, a campus weekly that averages about ten pages, mostly advertisements. I wanted to write back and say, "Quite the honor! It will be a step up from columns devoted to campus parties, singing groups, and complaints about dining-hall food." I chuckled at my own joke, but in the end the joke was on me. The campus journal he was referring to was the highly respected *Grosely Quarterly Review*, a peer-reviewed academic journal that was read by only a few people, but all of them were my colleagues.

The essay's publication forced the university to undergo an investigation, which is ongoing. My department chair suggested that I seek out letters attesting to my scholarship and moral character. As embarrassing as it was, I decided to reach out to my colleague in Connecticut, whom I considered a friend.

At first he was appalled to hear of my troubles, but when I began describing aspects of my pedagogical approach—namely making the subject matter more personal—he didn't seem to understand. "You mean, you sometimes conflate your own experience with the topic at hand in order to make a point?" His voice rose and I even thought it might be quivering, and I found myself on the defensive. My convoluted response only served to upset him further.

"That sounds a hell of a lot like lying," he said before hanging up.

My wife, who has been my greatest support throughout this ordeal, suggested that instead of calling out of the blue I should first write down what happened and provide a detailed rationale. "It's a lot to take in," she said. When I asked her if she believed that I had misrepresented myself, she responded, "Aren't we all guilty of self-mythologizing?"

"Does that mean yes or no?"

"Just write it out," she said.

So here it is, a brief explanation of my predicament. It probably goes without saying that my seminar on Latino gangs has been suspended indefinitely, which is just fine with me. When all this blows over, I'm going back to demographic shifts and treaties.

How I Broke Up with the Mayor

—〰—

for Artemio Pimentel

THE MAYOR AND I shared a change jar. I rarely left my room, let alone bought anything, so I never had much change, but the Mayor still said it was our change jar. When it was full we would drive to the Coinstar machine at the supermarket. The Mayor would ask that I carry the jar and that I place the coins in the machine. He said it wouldn't look right if the people of our city saw their mayor exchanging coins for cash. I thought to say, "What do they expect the mayor to do with his change, then?" But I understood what he meant. The machine was really loud, and people would turn around to see who was making such a racket. It was embarrassing. But I was happy to dump the change into the machine. Who cared if I was trying to get some extra cash to get through the month? As the coins clinked and clanged, I would turn around and see the Mayor about fifty feet away, pretending to inspect produce. When I finished I'd walk over and hand the voucher to the Mayor. Then we'd bring our voucher to the cashier and get cash, usually between fifty and seventy-five dollars. The Mayor would always count out the bills, then he would put them in his pocket and tell me, "This is our wine and cracker allotment." I didn't complain. I certainly drank and ate my fair share. It was always a good day when we exchanged our coin jar. Maybe because I felt as if the Mayor needed me, and how many people can say that?

The Mayor always made funny sounds. They were a combination of a squeal and a hum, more befitting a six-year-old than a politician. I wonder if his fiancé knows that about him. He might be ashamed to make the noises in front of her. He wasn't ashamed in front of me. I was his trusted confidant. I lived in the back in-law house and we shared the kitchen, and even though I wasn't technically allowed in the rest of the house, I still went in there when he wasn't home. Usually because I needed to check my e-mail on his computer, or steal a roll of toilet paper or a packet of saltine crackers, both of which he always kept in abundance in the hallway closet, or rifle through his mail looking for any letters addressed to me, mostly letters of rejection from agents and publishers and small literary journals. I used to wonder if he would grow angry with me if he found me in his part of the house, but I didn't think so because the Mayor was very rarely angry with anyone. It's what made him a good politician. Everything rolled off his back, even when people insulted him or accused him of corruption.

The Mayor knew I was a writer. Or at least he knew that that's what I did all day in the back house. I hadn't published anything yet, and the Mayor knew that, but he wasn't like most people who don't consider someone a writer until they publish, which I thought fair of him because if he had told me that he was a politician who had never held political office I guess I would've been far less forgiving. The Mayor had been a politician for most of his life. I once asked him how he got into politics and he proceeded, almost mechanically, to list every position he'd held since student-body vice president in the fourth grade. The Mayor didn't like to talk about politics. He preferred to discuss love and relationships, and sometimes, in moments of great vulnerability, he wanted to talk about the existence of an afterlife. But mostly we stuck to love and relationships, which was just fine with me. I didn't know any-thing about politics. I didn't know much about love and rela-tionships either, but I had read a lot of romance novels and those served me well during our late-night conversations. The Mayor was a poor sleeper. And when he couldn't sleep he liked to talk to someone, and what's more convenient than the guy who lives in back? The Mayor would step outside to smoke a Parliament, wearing a purple latex glove so his fingers wouldn't smell like cigarette, and he would whistle for me. I responded to that whistle like a faithful dog, springing out of bed ready to accompany my master. I understand that this description doesn't represent me well, so I'll clarify: a writer's master is his subject—he is a slave to stories, especially those shared late at night over bottles of wine and saltine crackers. So yes, I heard that whistle and I sprung out of bed, giddy with excitement as I put on my slippers and robe and joined the Mayor in his som-nambulant musings on love, heartbreak, and the hereafter.

The Mayor was never melancholy, he just liked melancholic subjects of conversation. In fact, I am more prone to melan-cholia than the Mayor, but he always had a way of getting me out of my moods. He would make those funny noises, and it was hard not to crack a smile. It was as though we shared a secret, and a secret is a remarkable thing when it's shared with the mayor of your city. If he was just some random guy I had to share a kitchen with who made strange squealing sounds and smoked outside with a purple glove on and kept me up all night lamenting the ones who got away, I would've moved out after a month. But he wasn't just some random guy. He was the Mayor. And to my mind, that's all that needs to be said. Sometimes, when we tired of talking, he would turn on the television and we would watch *SpongeBob SquarePants* together. The show made him die with laughter, and he would always glance over at me to make sure I was dying of laughter too. He was so earnest in his enjoyment of SpongeBob's antics that I couldn't help but share in his enthusiasm. It wasn't so hard once I got past the fact that it was a talking sponge. There were some genuinely funny parts. Like a lot of cartoons now, it operates on several levels. I wish I could say that the Mayor laughed only at the material directed at a more mature audience. When we didn't watch *Spongebob SquarePants*, we watched *Mama's Family*. That was harder to endure. It's a show centered around a grouchy, sharp-tongued old matriarch named Mama played by an actress who's not really old, she's just wearing a gray wig and glasses. The Mayor would tape this show and watch it every evening, and sometimes he would rewatch shows he had taped. I think he knew I didn't like *Mama's Family*, because after finishing a good long laugh he would sigh and look over at me and say, "What would the people of our city think, huh? The Mayor laughing at *Mama's Family*." I wanted to add, "And *SpongeBob SquarePants*," but he didn't seem to think being mayor and enjoying cartoons were incongruous.

The Mayor and I also had a dog together. I mean, it was the Mayor's dog, his sister gave it to him, but because my front yard was the Mayor's backyard, it was as though we shared him. The dog was a brown Labrador, and the Mayor's sister said his name was Cocoa, but the Mayor decided that that was no name for a male dog and decided to call him Volvo, after the car, which he thought was masculine. Because the Mayor possessed a slight accent, which he always chalked up to learning English as a second language, he didn't pronounce his hard o's. So I thought he was calling the dog "Vulva," and his rationale didn't make any sense. Anyway, at first I was a little annoyed because Volvo was just a puppy and a brown Lab to boot, which meant that he could wreak havoc. The dog dug out all my plants from their pots, chewed through my screen door, and practically gnawed through the patio chair where I enjoyed sipping my midafternoon coffee. Not to mention the fact that the dog peed and shat all over my front yard (the Mayor's backyard). All of this I dealt with quietly. I picked up the shit. I repotted my plants. I bought dog-repellant spray. But by far the worst was that as soon as the Mayor left every morning to go to city hall, the dog started whining until the Mayor returned later that evening. It didn't matter that I was close by. It didn't matter that I would stop writing and come out to throw a tennis ball. The puppy didn't care about me. He only cared about the Mayor, and the Mayor was gone, and he would whine until the Mayor returned. It made it very difficult to concentrate. I finally had to say something. One night as the Mayor was smoking his Parliament with his purple glove on, his arms folded in a debonair manner, he heard me out, nodding his head understandingly, and when I finished, he said to me, "Well, should we get rid of our dog?"

This was the first time he had referred to Volvo as *our* dog. It made the situation very different. Suddenly, I shared a living thing with the Mayor. I couldn't help but turn to Volvo, who, of course, was gazing up at us excitedly, his tongue hanging out, waiting for us to play with him.

"No, I don't want to get rid of him!" I exclaimed. "Of course not. Not at all. I just feel that maybe we could spend some time, perhaps, together, training our dog."

A smile came to the Mayor's lips. "I know how to train dogs," he said.

"You do?" I asked.

"Of course," he said. "I grew up with dogs."

He went inside the house and returned a few minutes later carrying the day's newspaper. He rolled it up tightly, the entire time looking at Volvo as the puppy looked up at him with adoring, expectant eyes. The Mayor suddenly lunged for Volvo, grabbed him by the collar, and violently dragged him over to my potted plants. Then, one by one, he shoved the dog's nose into the dirt. "You see that? You see that?" the Mayor said through clenched teeth. Volvo whined pitifully, the entire time looking up at me as if to say, *Why? Why did you have to tell him?* And then the Mayor swatted Volvo with the rolled up newspaper with such vigor that to this day I cannot view a newspaper without hearing Volvo's pitiful cries. I must've cried out in shock or horror or both, because the Mayor finally stopped and, in between breaths, said, "What's the matter with you?"

Gasping for very different reasons, I said, "You're hurting him!"

The Mayor started to laugh. "Hurting him? It's a rolled-up newspaper." And with that he swatted me on the arm, and he was right, it didn't hurt in the least. So that's how we trained our dog, or at least that's how we tried. Volvo just wasn't very cooperative. We finally tied him up to a tree in the far backyard, where he was always getting tangled up in his leash and whining or howling until he was freed. It wasn't long before the neighbors started to complain. One day I came home and Volvo was gone. I never asked what happened to him, and the Mayor never told me. I just figured the Mayor knew tons of people, so he must have found Volvo a good home.

One late night, the Mayor whistled for me and I quickly jumped out of bed and emerged from my back house, expecting to find him with his purple glove on, smoking a cigarette. Instead, he held a container of salt. "You want to see something?" he asked. The excitement in his voice was palpable. It was chilly and I'd forgotten my robe, so I went back inside to get it. When I came back out he had his purple glove on and was smoking a cigarette. "What are we going to do?" I asked, tightening the sash of my robe. "You'll see," he said. When he finished his cigarette he put it out in one of my potted plants and snapped off the latex glove as if he'd just performed successful heart surgery. I followed him down the driveway and to the front yard. He pushed aside some shrubs and crept toward the large front window. He looked as if he were spying on his empty living room. He beckoned me closer. I still couldn't figure out what we were doing. We stared into his living room, the television on, the lamp above the dining table casting a golden glow, his cell phone resting precariously on the arm of the couch. I half expected his doppelgänger to emerge, or rather, the real Mayor to emerge and for me to realize I was with his doppelgänger. But then he raised the container of salt and snickered. That was when I saw the object of his attention. Crawling, leaving a long path of slime up the window, was a snail. The Mayor's snicker broke into an outright giggle as he slowly lifted the salt container over the snail. I don't know why he did it so slowly; it wasn't as if he had to catch the snail unawares. Maybe to prolong our anticipation. But I had no idea what I was anticipating, I just knew it wasn't good. Still, I never expected the sheer violence of what followed. He poured the salt onto the snail and it frothed and shriveled up instantaneously like a witch doused with water, then it fell dead to the ground. The Mayor started laughing, and I tried to laugh with him, but my stomach was in my throat. I could hardly breathe, let alone laugh. The Mayor's face became serious. I think he misread my shock for disapproval, and he said, somewhat somberly, "I guess there's still a kid in all of us, even the mayor." Then he slapped me on the arm and headed back inside. I followed him, and we spent the rest of the night watching *Mama's Family*. I couldn't forget what I'd seen. Something about the swiftness of the snail's death reminded me of the preciousness of life, how just like that it can end, brutally! The Mayor must've sensed my thoughts, because after we finished watching several episodes he decided to expound on his second favorite topic: the existence of an afterlife.

The Mayor really, really wanted to believe that we didn't just die, that there was a heaven or that we were born again, reincarnated, something, anything, as long as we didn't just die. The Mayor stopped going to church when he went away to college, and even though I never asked him outright, I sensed that once he was done with religion he was also done with God. So he was an agnostic for sure, maybe an atheist, but he was also a solipsist, so the thought of him, the Mayor, not existing in any shape or form was just too much to bear. Our conversations were always the same, always circuitous, and some nights I told him that I didn't think there was an afterlife, which caused him great consternation, so then the next time I would tell him that I did, in fact, believe there was an afterlife, but then he would so desperately want to know for sure that he would pick apart my lackluster defense. It was a lose-lose situation, which is why I always tried to steer the conversation back to love and relationships. This was relatively easy: I would just start talking about my relationships, and he would very quickly become inspired and cut me off to talk about his own.

The Mayor's relationships usually followed the same trajectory. A hopeless romantic, he'd meet a woman, fall head over heels in love, then the woman would inevitably fail to live up to the ideal he had created. What followed would be a series of what he called "red flags": she liked candy too much and didn't exercise; she didn't care for politics; she was too materialistic; she didn't like to cook; her apartment was a disaster; she had too many cats; she lived too far away; she took too long to get ready; she expected him to open her car door; she didn't like *SpongeBob SquarePants*—these are just a few that I remember. It didn't take much for the Mayor to fall out of love, because he wasn't really in love in the first place; he just convinced himself that he was. Either way, the disappointment was the same. The Mayor heartbroken was a sight to see. He'd call in sick to city hall, pull out bottles of tequila, and play romantic Mexican ballads on an endless loop at full volume. He wouldn't shave or comb his hair, and he'd smoke his Parliaments inside the house and *without* the purple glove. It broke my heart to watch him suffer so. Still, these were some of my happiest moments with the Mayor. How many people can say they were with the mayor of their city at his most vulnerable, drinking tequila, listening to Vicente Fernández? When he shed a tear, I shed a tear. When he cried out, "When will I find her?" I cried out, "It will happen someday soon!" When he cried out, "I deserve this!" I cried out, "How can you say such a thing?" What's strange is that these bouts of depression usually occurred before the relationship even ended. The Mayor never actually broke up with any of these women. In that regard he was a coward. He would just stop calling them back, and either they would get the hint and quietly go away, or they would send desperate e-mails and text messages or leave voicemails spewing venom and break up with him themselves. This was one instance where the Mayor and I disagreed. How those women suffered as they waited for his phone call! I told him that he had to put them out of their misery. He wasn't doing them any favors. And the Mayor would say, "I can't do it. It's just too hard." The man runs a city, but he can't end a relationship. So we reached a compromise. I would compose the e-mail breaking up with the girlfriend, and he would agree to press "send." In fact, knowing the ins and outs of the relationships, familiar with the Mayor's voice, and coming from a position of empathy, I was probably the best person to write these e-mails. I saw it as my role to soften the blow. They may be heartbroken, but I could give them an ember of hope, just enough to pick themselves up and continue anew, someday. More selfishly, I also saw these e-mails as literary exercises, and once on a whim I collected them all together, gave it a title—"Women Whom I Have Broken Up with for the Mayor"—and sent it to a whole slew of obscure literary journals. I never expected to hear back.

The beginning of the end of my time with the Mayor began as so many other nights had before. We were seated in his living room, the fire crackling. He was seated on the long couch, a pillow cushion on his lap. I sat on the adjacent shorter couch. The living room was dark except for the light provided by the fire and the flat-screen television, which was on pause, leaving Mama of *Mama's Family* with her eyes half-open, about to say something. We were eating saltines and were on our second bottle of wine, a cheap, tinny Merlot that I could feel on my teeth. I couldn't see the Mayor's face. I just knew he was preoccupied and quieter than usual. Earlier, he had smoked almost an entire pack of cigarettes, and his beckoning whistle didn't have the same energy. Still, he had told me, "I have a story for you. This one you'll have to write down. Otherwise no one will believe it." This is something he would say from time to time, and I always took his words to heart. So desperate for validation, it made me feel as if someone believed in me. I promised him I would write down every detail.

In the darkness, I heard the Mayor's voice.

"Do you remember Berta?" he asked.

"Of course I remember her," I responded. Of all the girl-friends I broke up with for the Mayor, she was the hardest. She was really the best of the bunch. Her only "red flag" was her name. The Mayor didn't think it was the right kind of name for a politician's wife. His colleagues pronounced it Burr-ta, and it grated on him to no end. That, and she only liked art-house and foreign films (the Mayor's taste ran more toward romantic comedies). She also spoke English with a heavy accent; sometimes she was incomprehensible. She was a US citizen because she was born here, but she'd lived most of her life in some small rancho in Michoacán.

"Well, she has me backed into a corner," he said.

"What kind of corner?" I asked.

The Mayor was quiet for a long time. Then he sighed and said, "Seriously, you gotta write this one down. I can hardly believe it myself. You'll have a best seller on your hands, I swear to God."

"Yes," I said. I was practically holding my breath in anticipation for his story to begin.

The Mayor explained that Berta had called him the night before and told him she had some information he might want to keep quiet. She told him she would give him the information in exchange for a visa for her cousin. She wanted him to meet her at her temporary home, Los Solos—loosely translated as the Lonely Men—a cluster of trailers for workers on Peterson Farms. The Mayor had no intention of getting a visa for the cousin, something he had no power to do but that everyone assumed he did, but he wanted to see what compromising information she had.

"She's blackmailing you?!" I exclaimed. It didn't fit my idea of kindhearted Berta.

"And that's not all," the Mayor responded. "Berta knows that I didn't write the e-mail to break up with her. She thought something sounded strange about it, so she printed out all our previous correspondence, including our text messages, and she brought them to a forensic linguist, who could tell right off that someone else had written the final e-mail."

"How the hell would Berta find a forensic linguist?" I asked.

"The point is she did. And she asked if it was you who'd written it."

"Me?"

"Yes, and so I told her that you had."

"You did?!" I exclaimed.

"Yes, I'm sorry. I felt as though I had no choice. But now she's out to ruin you too."

"Ruin me? But I didn't do anything wrong! Why is she upset with me?"

"She's not upset. She just felt wronged and wants revenge for what we did."

"For what *we* did? I just composed the e-mail!" I said.

"Well, apparently there's some stuff in there she didn't like," he said.

I couldn't believe what I was hearing. I was now polishing off one saltine after another in between gulps of wine. The Mayor told me to calm down. "We're going to handle this. Berta is out of control, but if we're not careful she's going to bring us both down. Both of us," he said. "Our careers are at stake."

I didn't know how Berta could bring down my career. I didn't even have a career. And if I did, as a writer, I didn't see how a writer's career could be brought down other than by charges of plagiarism. I then wondered if I had plagiarized something. Maybe the forensic linguist had discovered something I wasn't even aware of.

"Let's go to Los Solos together," the Mayor said. "I need your help."

"What can I do?"

"Look, if I could handle this alone I would, but I'm the Mayor. I can't just be showing up at the Peterson Farms work camp at ten o'clock at night."

The Mayor asked me to drive because he said someone might recognize his car. I told him that I'd probably had too many glasses of wine and maybe I wasn't the safest driver at that point. He just chuckled and said, "It's just a couple of straight country roads." On the way out to Los Solos I asked the Mayor what damaging information Berta could possibly have on him, and he told me that it was personal stuff, nothing political, and that he had to protect his family, his mother more specifically, but he didn't elaborate beyond that and we drove the rest of the way in silence.

When we were within a hundred yards of Los Solos and I could see the porch lights off in the distance, the Mayor instructed me to pull to the side of the road and to turn off my headlights. Then he pulled a ski mask and a crowbar out of his jacket pocket.

"What the hell are those?" I practically shrieked.

"A ski mask and a crowbar," he said.

"What do we need that for? You've got to be joking!"

I could barely make out the Mayor's face. "I need your help," I heard him say in the plaintive, vulnerable voice that he used during our discussions about the existence of an afterlife. "You're the only one I can count on, really. You're more than just my friend, you're like—you're like—well, I'll say it. You're like my consigliere. You take care of business, you're no-nonsense, you're dependable. A man like me doesn't get any-where without someone like you beside him." And with that he handed me the ski mask and crowbar.

I have to admit, I flushed with pride upon hearing this. I had always thought of myself as the random guy in the backyard who drank a lot of wine and ate all the Mayor's saltines and liked to listen to his stories, so to suddenly be called the Mayor's consigliere by the Mayor himself gave my life unin-tended purpose. I think if he had asked me to murder someone right then I would've considered it. But he didn't. He just asked that I "give her a little scare."

"Who?" I asked.

"Berta, who else?"

"Berta? But I can't do that, she's—"

"She's blackmailing us. She's not the sweet Berta we knew, okay? And we're not hurting her, we're just showing her that if she wants to play with matches, she can expect a fire. She'll back off with a little scare, trust me." Then he sighed and looked at the crowbar in his hands as if he was contemplating doing the deed himself even though he had so much to lose. I couldn't let him do it.

"How am I supposed to scare her?" I asked.

"Put on this mask, take this crowbar, and break the window to the second trailer on the far left. That's where we were supposed to meet her. She'll get the message."

"What are you going to do?"

"I'll be waiting here," he said. Then he placed his hand on my shoulder and said, with what I guess was supposed to be an Italian accent, "Mi consigliere!"

It wasn't until I was outside walking toward Los Solos that I wondered why the otherwise reputable mayor of our city would liken himself to a mafia boss. I was very conflicted at that moment. My loyalties were with the Mayor, of course, but I didn't want to scare Berta. She was so beautiful and sweet, and she deserved someone who appreciated her, and I told her as much in my breakup letter. Why couldn't she just stay out of his life? Didn't she know not to mess with men in power?

It was cold, and I briefly reflected on the warm fire I had been sitting in front of just a half hour before. I still felt drunk. Through the holes of my ski mask I could see my breath in the air. I placed one hand in my pocket. The other grasped the crowbar, which felt like an icicle. Why did I need a crowbar? I could just as well throw a rock. In fact, I thought that might be safer. I could remain far enough away from the trailer. But then, my ability to throw was never very good. I'd probably miss, and if I did hit it, there was no telling who might be sleeping underneath the window. What if the rock should hit them? What if they should be struck by a shard of glass? Wouldn't that happen with the crowbar too? Suddenly, I was awash in horror stories of window breaking turned tragic. Blindness, gaping wounds, and death all became possibilities. What would my defense be? The Mayor made me do it? These labor camps were usually teeming with people. I figured ten occupants were sleeping in each trailer. There was almost zero chance I'd not hit someone with a flying shard. What was Berta doing living in a trailer full of fieldworkers, anyway? Berta, sweet, beautiful Berta. I once imagined the two of us, curled on the Mayor's couch in front of a fire, watching art-house films. And here I was about to inflict harm on her. No, I was just going to give her a little scare . . . I should turn back, I should really turn back . . . Horrible thoughts continued to race through my mind when I heard something behind me. I turned just in time to see a dark, shadowy figure hit me across the forehead with something hard, possibly a crowbar.

When I awoke it was morning and I was shaking uncontrollably. I was lying in wet grass. A dog was licking my forehead. I tried pushing it away, but it was as if I didn't have control of my limbs. I couldn't move my legs. I couldn't move my arms. I couldn't even find the muscles to rise from the ground. All I could do was shake. So the dog kept licking my forehead. I don't think I'd ever felt so cold in my life. I wouldn't have been surprised if I'd looked down and discovered I was naked. I wasn't. I had all my clothes on except for my ski mask. What had happened to my ski mask? More importantly, where was the Mayor? I recalled being hit on the head. It briefly flashed through my mind that it was the Mayor who did it, but I quickly dispelled the idea. Why would he do such a thing? Why would anyone do such a thing? I guess I was the intruder carrying a crowbar. Speaking of which, where was the crowbar? Suddenly I realized I knew the dog. It was our brown Lab, Volvo! He wasn't a puppy anymore. He looked the same, just bigger. He even seemed happy to see me, and for a brief moment I was happy for him. It looked like he had ample room to roam, and there was no leash to get tangled in. I was starting to get some feeling back in my arms and legs. I rose from the ground and felt an excruciating pain in my head. I wondered if I had a concussion. I touched my forehead. I was still bleeding. *Good God, I had been left to die*, I thought. I looked around. I wasn't near the road anymore. Los Solos trailer camp was off in the distance.

When I was finally able to stand I saw that my car was gone. I don't know why I expected to find it there. I wondered if the Mayor drove off when he saw me attacked. Maybe the Mayor had been attacked too. Was he the real target? Was I simply collateral damage? Then I wondered what Volvo was doing there at Los Solos. Had the Mayor given him to Berta, to one of the workers? All these questions made my head hurt. I started walking back toward the city. It took me two hours to reach home, and Volvo followed me the entire way. When I arrived at the house my car was in the driveway, but the Mayor's car was gone. I entered through the back door and found some leftover dog treats we'd never thrown out. I gave a few to Volvo. Then I went back inside and called out the Mayor's name. He didn't answer. From the kitchen, I knocked on the door that led to the rest of the house. I opened it and peeked my head into the living room. It was exactly as we had left it the night before. Our glasses of wine were on the coffee table, the pillows were in disarray, and half a packet of saltines remained on the arm of the sofa. I was famished. I picked up the packet and dug out a handful of crackers and stuffed them in my mouth. As I was trying to swallow, I noticed that there was a book on the couch, half covered with a throw pillow. I picked up the pillow and didn't recognize the plain white cover. The Mayor never read anything except books with flashy covers and titles containing phrases like "effective management" and "principles of leadership." This book cover looked like it was printed in someone's garage. I leaned closer, my head aching as I squinted to read the title. *Lower Valley College Review: A Journal of Literature and Art*. I picked it up and scanned the front and back covers. The name sounded familiar. I was sure I had submitted something there, but I couldn't remember what. Sometimes when journals reject you they put you on their subscription list as a form of consolation. I turned the book over to where the Mayor had it opened. It took me a moment to process what I saw. My heart was beating. I had to sit down. For the first time in my life my name was in print. I had been published! Why hadn't I been informed? I wanted to cry out in joy, I wanted to run around the block holding the journal above my head. I wanted to call my asshole brother the banker and let him know that I hadn't "wasted Mom and Dad's hard work" after all. But then I noticed what story had been published, and my joy quickly turned to dread. It was "Women Whom I Have Broken Up with for the Mayor."

"I probably wouldn't have paid attention if you'd picked a less obvious title," I heard the Mayor say.

I looked up, startled.

I hadn't even heard him come in. He was standing in the kitchen doorway.

"Is that Volvo in the backyard?" he asked as he approached the sofas. He plopped down on the smaller couch, placed his feet on the arm, and situated one of the pillows underneath his head.

I nodded. "He followed me home."

"Imagine my surprise," the Mayor began. "I'm opening my mail and I accidentally open one of your letters. I was about to seal it back up when I spotted something about *me* in the letter. It was congratulating you for your innovative story, called 'Women Whom I Have Broken Up with for the Mayor.' I thought to myself, 'There's no way those could be about me. Surely my friend wouldn't betray me like that. Surely, he wouldn't be dumb enough to publish my personal letters without changing a name, a date, not one detail—'"

"I didn't think they'd publish them!" I said.

He ignored me. "So I waited for the journal to come, and sure enough I turn to your story and there's my life, my feelings, my heart . . . for everyone to see."

"But you always told me to write down your stories," I said, swallowing hard.

The Mayor started to laugh. "You can't be serious."

"Yes. You always said it."

"Isn't that just something you say to a writer? I didn't think you'd actually write down my stories! Who wants their dirty laundry aired in public?"

"I thought you meant it," I said.

The Mayor looked at me as though unable to decide whether I was naïve or just plain stupid.

"I really thought you meant it," I said again.

The Mayor chuckled. "And here I thought you were the smart one."

"I mean, I sat here for hours listening to your stories."

The Mayor scoffed and shook his head. "So you're telling me that you actually thought I wanted you to write my stories and then publish them for all the world to see."

"Yes."

"Well, in the future, don't. And now you know what will happen to you if you publish any more of my personal life."

"What do you mean?" I asked. But then it hit me. "So you *are* the one who clubbed me over the head?"

The Mayor laughed, a laugh that reminded me of the giggling fit he had after dousing the snail in salt.

"How could you do such a thing?" I cried.

"*I* didn't do it," he said. "I had one of my dad's workers do it. I told him to keep watch because there'd been some suspicious activity in the area. I gave him fifty bucks to be extra vigilant. I had to prove a point."

"Prove what point?"

"Not to use me and my life for your own benefit," he said.

"Couldn't you have just told me?" I asked, but as soon the question was out of my mouth I realized that after personally ending at least six of his relationships I should know that directness was not the Mayor's strong point.

He picked up the publication and stared at it intently, frowning as though reliving his initial disappointment. "These are my letters verbatim, aren't they?" He opened it to a page and held it up for me to see. I squinted my eyes and tried to make out the words. It was the page containing Berta's letter. Suddenly, it occurred to me that the whole situation with her had been a ruse.

"Why Berta?" I asked.

"Why Berta what?"

"She never even called, did she? Why did you say she was blackmailing you?"

"Because she was the perfect bait."

"Why would you think that?" I asked, my voice incredulous, though of course he had been right.

"Just read what you wrote right here," the Mayor said, tossing the book onto my lap. It bounced off my leg and fell onto the floor. I didn't need to reread Berta's letter to know why the Mayor chose her. Except for the part ending the relationship, the letter could have been a declaration of love.

"So not only did you use me, but you also coveted my girlfriend."

"I didn't *covet* her. I was supposed to write as if I were you—"

The Mayor raised his hand to silence me. I thought he was going to say something, but he remained quiet.

I sighed and leaned my head against the back of the couch. I was in a lot of pain. I hadn't even washed the blood off my forehead. I waited for the Mayor to say more. I expected him to tell me to pack my things and get out. But after a moment of silence, the Mayor reached for the remote and turned on the television. Soon we were watching an episode of *SpongeBob SquarePants*, and the Mayor was giggling as if all was back to normal. I rose to leave, and he asked, "Where are you going? You don't want to watch *SpongeBob*?"

I didn't last much longer at the Mayor's house. Not because he tried to have me killed. We got past that. Even though probably no one read my first published story except for my parents and the editors of the *Lower Valley College Review* (all of them students at the community college), I saw just how stupid I was to think that the Mayor would want me to write his stories. He was a public figure, and that was all the more reason why his personal life had to remain private. He had let me in, and I had betrayed that trust. I deserved to get hit in the head with a crowbar (it was actually a 2×4). I understood that now. And maybe one day we would've returned to how we once

were, sitting in the living room drinking wine and eating saltines, the Mayor telling me his stories, and this time I
would've known not to write them down even though he said,
"You gotta write this down." I learned it's just something people say.

Maybe I would've returned to being the Mayor's confidant,
his consigliere, but we never got our chance. Not too long after,
the Mayor met his trophy wife, and his love and relationship
woes ended. He was happy and he no longer worried so much
about the existence of an afterlife. He didn't need me anymore,
I guess. But he didn't tell me this directly. Instead, he wrote me
an e-mail informing me that his fiancé was moving in soon and
she didn't feel comfortable having "some guy living in the back
and sharing their kitchen." I knew this day would come. After
I read the e-mail I rose from my computer, and, without thinking to go inside and confront the Mayor, I spent the rest of the
day packing my things. I would leave without saying good-bye,
I decided. After all the countless hours we spent hashing out
life's travails, all the advice I'd given him, all the hours wasted
watching his stupid television programs, he didn't even have
the decency to whistle for me one last time. I was angry.
Scorned! I felt as though he had taken a part of my life and
poured an entire container of salt over it, the years shriveling
and frothing and withering into nothingness. My anger grew. I
wanted to take something from him. I stepped outside and
called Volvo to my side.

"Come here, boy! You want to go for a ride?"

The dog approached as he always did, heavy pawed and
tongue wagging. I petted him and he licked my hand. Then I
grabbed hold of his collar, and he must have sensed what was
about to happen, because he immediately began whimpering
and pulling away, his paws slipping on the smooth pavement.
I was about to yank on his collar when I saw the fear in his big
brown eyes. He didn't want to come with me, and I didn't have
the heart to force him.

So I did something that I'm not proud of: I stole our change
jar, which was almost full.

The Twins

—❦—

for Will Goldsmith

THE TWINS WERE such pitiful creatures. Motherless. Shirtless. They looked like they ate nothing but Cheetos and the unripe oranges they pilfered from the Maestro's tree. I would watch them from the many windows in the Maestro's house and studio. They were always together, tromping back and forth, off to find adventure and mischief, mostly mischief. They had beady blue eyes, pasty white skin, and a few freckles across the nose. At first you couldn't tell them apart, but only at first. One was slightly taller, slightly narrower, with an arched eyebrow, scars on his lip and chin, and a tooth askew. The other was more confident; he walked with his head held high and his fists always clenched. He was prone to mood swings. He was the leader of the two, the one who made the first leap, but in truth they were two ends of the same beast, both lost without the other. Whenever I called the cops on them, they would take away one, leaving the other, and it would break my heart to see him so, walking back and forth, head hung low, his gaze not rising above his feet, as though he were looking for his brother in his own gait. A few days would pass, a week, and the brother would be released from juvenile hall, a patrol car dropping him off in front of the apartments, looking as if he'd just hitched a ride, and upon seeing each other the twins' faces would light up; they'd come to life again, as if finally able to breathe. They'd run toward one another, looking as if they were about to embrace and never let go or proclaim how much they missed each other, but instead they would sock each other in the arm, in the stomach, or engage in a prolonged slap fight, covering each other in red marks. Love pats, maybe, warped displays of affection; I don't know the ways of brothers, let alone twins. They would soon return to tromping around, looking for adventure and mischief, and it was a sight to see the happiness on their faces. I would vow never to call the police again. I would not be the one to separate them.

They were such troublemakers though. They did such horrible things. Some of it was harmless, boys being boys, but some of it wasn't. Like the time they caught twenty-odd frogs in the creek, hung them from the clothesline, and then spent the afternoon picking them off with a pellet gun. Or when I saw them taunting the pit bull at the corner junkyard. Protected by a chain link fence topped with barbed wire, the twins thought nothing of wiling away a few hours throwing rocks at the dog. Later I learned they had enraged the poor thing until it suffered a heart attack. They started small brush fires. They stole cigarettes and beer from the corner store and smoked and drank until they barfed their brains out; I could hear them just over the fence, moaning for mercy. They would crawl into the abandoned cars in the back lot and masturbate to brassiere ads found in the Sunday newspaper. They stole the Maestro's unripe oranges and threw them at passing cars. They left nails and tacks in the road. They followed Ms. Edward's daughter, who suffered from cerebral palsy, and imitated her labored movements on her way home from the post office; when she cried out, "Thaawp, Thaaawp," they broke into hysterics. They found a stray kitten and put a bag over its head, sealed it with a rubber band, and threw it into the Maestro's pool. That was where I found it, floating. I had to fish it out with a skimmer meant for leaves. The kitten lay heavy on the netting, and I could barely make out what it was. Not until I removed the rubber band and the plastic bag from its head. Then I held its limp body in my hands and began to sob. I heard giggles from a tree, and I looked up to find the twins, shirtless as always, their noses scrunched up, their beady eyes lost in the squint of their laughter. I wondered how long they had waited for this moment, for their misdeed to be discovered.

"How could you do such a thing?" I cried, ashamed of my tears.

"Fuck you, you fag," one of them said.

Then like some strange breed of monkey they swung from one branch to another and quickly lowered themselves from the tree and disappeared. I couldn't leave the kitten there on the pathway. I found a shovel and dug a hole in the far back, behind the Maestro's studio, then retrieved the kitten, wrapped it in a blanket—providing too late the warmth and protection it needed—and buried it. Still in shock, my hands trembling, I called the cops. They arrived hours later, a fat old one and skinny young one, both obviously annoyed at having to drive out to the country for a dead kitten. I explained the ghastly nature of its death. They were unmoved. They simply told me that because I'd already buried it they couldn't verify that a crime had indeed been committed. Hearing this, I got choked up all over again.

"You could dig it up," the fat cop suggested.

"Hasn't it already been violated enough?" I exclaimed.

The cops both seemed to be holding back their laughter, as if they'd never seen a grown man cry over a dead kitten.

"Look," the fat cop said, speaking as if to a child, "even if the cat was killed like you say, what proof do you have that the twins are the ones who did it?"

"Who else would do such a thing? Those kids harm animals for sport."

"Well, like we tell everybody here in town, if you caught them on video or something, or more than one person saw them

143

doing it, then that's one thing, but we can't just arrest them based on your assumption. If you're really worried about the animals in the area, I suggest you call protective services."

He gave me his card and they left.

I was house-sitting for the Maestro, the great painter and my former mentor. After my wife died, I plunged into a deep depression. I didn't want to be in our home anymore, so I'd go to the studio all day, but I didn't want to be in the studio either, because it was merely the dark and dusty corner of an abandoned plastics factory overcrowded with junk. I used to revel in its squalor, but after her sickness and rapid decline, emptiness reminded me of death, and I was haunted by the hollow sounds that echoed throughout the day. I visited the Maestro one afternoon and told him that I couldn't sleep, I couldn't eat, and I couldn't work in my dark, dusty corner anymore. He too had lost his wife some years back, and so I asked him, "How long will this last, Maestro?" And he told me that it never goes away, that he always has the feeling that his wife is just around the corner or in the other room, or that any moment he'll hear the car in the driveway and she'll honk her horn for him to come help carry in groceries.

"It just gets easier somehow," he said. "And sometimes, too, it helps to have a change of location."

"I can't afford to go anywhere," I told him. And that was when he told me he was going to be in Europe for the year, teaching art in Florence, then later in Bordeaux. And then he told me a story I knew well, how his parents were migrant fieldworkers, and when they'd pick grapes and lay them out on paper trays to sun dry, they'd always take a few sheets for him to draw on. "I don't really want to go to Europe," he said, "but I do it for them. Because even in their wildest dreams they'd never imagine where those drawings on grape trays would lead me." I smiled at the Maestro, even as I wondered, "Why is he telling me this?" I'd heard his rags-to-relative-riches story a thousand times. I used to love hearing it, but now it only made me sad. Everything that was beautiful made me sad.

Everything that was ugly too. It goes without saying that I was a wreck. I left the Maestro and thought it would be a long time before I saw him again, but a few days later he called and said that the person who was going to house-sit for him fell through, and he wanted to know if I'd care to live there for the year. "You can use my studio, of course," he said. In truth, it felt like too much energy to move: to pack my stuff, to unpack my stuff, to figure out the workings of another home, to water his infinite amount of plants and flowers. But that was only the depression talking. I'd have been a fool not to accept the Maestro's offer.

The Maestro's house, a beautiful old Victorian painted beige with turquoise and rust trim, was full of light, every room painted a bright, bold color, the exact opposite of his monochromatic paintings. His work adorned the walls, large expressionistic portraits, along with a lifetime of photographs—old friends, the Maestro and his wife, their children as kids, their children now grown, their children with their families. There were hundreds of books stacked every which way. His wife used to keep them in alphabetical order and on the shelves, but that was one of the first things to give way. Otherwise the Maestro kept everything as his wife liked it. On my first day alone in the house I spent an hour or more in each room, exploring every detail as though compelled to learn the entire history of the place before allowing myself to inhabit it. It felt like a museum; I couldn't just plop down on a sofa and kick my feet up. I had to learn the place, and when I was done learning the house, I had to learn the studio, with its gigantic windows and beautiful light and paint-splattered floor. To the left of the Maestro's house was another old Victorian; to the right was a lot with three small duplexes painted a sickly avocado green with cracking brown trim. The lot was filled with junked cars lost in overgrown weeds. It was an eyesore, and the Maestro had tried with some success to block it with shrubbery and fences. The twins lived in one of the duplexes. On my first night in the Maestro's home I awoke to flashing red lights filtering through the guest bedroom's lace curtains. At first I thought I was having a nightmare, reliving the night the ambulances arrived to take away my wife for the last time. I lay there a minute before rising from bed to see what was going on. I pulled the curtain aside and saw a police car. As my eyes adjusted, I noticed in the porch light two small, shirtless boys huddled together. They were seated on the concrete porch, their arms apparently cuffed behind their backs. *Were the cops arresting these poor boys?* I wondered. I saw a cop talking to a wild-haired obese man who was also shirtless. He was waving his arms and alternating between grabbing his stringy hair and rubbing his enormous hairy belly. I couldn't hear what he was saying at first, but after a while I made out his blubbering: "I don't have any control over them! They don't listen to me!" I watched the scene for some time, disturbed but unable to turn away. Finally a cop walked over to the little boys, lifted them from the porch, escorted them into the police car, and drove off, leaving the wild-haired fat man alone to gripe to the moon about his children not listening to a damn thing he said. It was an altogether odd scene. I couldn't figure out why it was the children and not the fat drunk who were led away in handcuffs.

Two days later, I saw the boys return, again in a police car. I was watering the Maestro's plants and flowers along the side of the house. The twins were in the backseat, their heads barely visible above the window. The cop stepped out of the car and opened their door. One scooted out and then the other. I saw that they were older than I thought them to be the other night, eleven or twelve rather than seven or eight. They were still shirtless. The cop got back in the car and drove off, leaving the boys alone in the potholed gravel driveway. They turned to stare at me. I avoided their gaze, pretending to focus on the task at hand, but when I looked up I saw that they were still staring with their beady blue eyes. I smiled at them, but they didn't smile back. They just kept looking at me with a transfixed expression on their faces. I couldn't tell one from the other.

"Hello!" I said, to be friendly, and for lack of anything else to say.

They were quiet for some time before one of them said, "Where's the old man?"

"The old man?" I said. "You mean the Maestro?"

They looked at me, confused.

"I'm watching his house for him," I said.

They continued to look at me as though my presence confounded them.

"What are you doing?" the bolder one asked.

I chuckled. "Well, I'm watering," I said.

His eyes narrowed. "We used to help the old man water," he said.

"You did, is that right?" I said.

"Yeah, and you know what, he had us water these flowers over here on our side." He pointed at something on the other side of the white picket fence and then bent down as if he wanted me to see the flowers for myself.

"Oh, he didn't tell me about those," I said, walking toward them. I didn't really believe him, but I decided to play along. I wanted to be friendly.

The other brother remained still, his back erect, like a soldier standing at attention. He looked frightened.

"If you give me the hose," the talker said, "I'll water these flowers over here."

Without thinking, I released the spray-nozzle trigger and handed him the hose. Then I peered over the fence. As I suspected, there weren't any flowers. I peered farther. There was only weed grass along that entire side. In a somewhat patronizing tone, I said, "Now, just where were those flowers you helped water—" When I turned to him I saw that he was pointing the nozzle right at me. Up until he pulled the trigger I didn't really believe he would spray me. It was so unfathomable that I mistook it for impossible. In a matter of minutes, a child, fresh out of juvenile hall, just dropped off by a patrol car, interrupts my watering, attempts to trick me into handing him a hose, which I do for reasons I can't quite explain, then sprays me with it. But that's exactly what he did. He sprayed me, first in my face, and then when I said, "Hey, quit that!" and raised my forearms to protect myself, he sprayed me again, this time in my crotch. Then he tossed the hose, grabbed his brother's hand,

147

and they ran away giggling. I couldn't move I was so shocked. From a safe distance away, I heard the twin call out, "Look, he peed, he peed his pants!" I looked down and saw that my pants were indeed drenched. I went inside, more bewildered than anything else, and changed clothes.

I didn't return that evening to finish watering. I should have. The longer I stayed inside, the angrier I grew. My wife would've called it stewing. I could still see the hose lying where it was tossed onto the lawn. I didn't know what to do. I wanted revenge, but of course I knew better. Revenge? Against a child? I was the grown-up, I had to act like one, but all I could think about was catching that kid and demanding an apology. I knew that my wife would be laughing at me. "You were the dummy to hand him the hose!" she would say. And I probably would've laughed with her. But she wasn't around to say it any longer, so I was left to my curmudgeonly thoughts. Honestly, I wanted nothing more than to drench that kid with the nozzle on full blast.

My wife was a schoolteacher and she loved children, all children, no matter how rambunctious or devious. She would come home from school, tired but full of stories. She would tell me about each and every one of her students so that it felt as if I were there in the classroom with her. Her students consumed her. Even her dreams took place at school. I knew because she was a sleeptalker—not just fitful murmuring but full-on talking. When we were first together it would startle me, and I would try to wake her up or calm her or bring her back to bed, but she was an insistent sleeptalker; she didn't wish to be interrupted, and she would shrug off my caresses. At times she would rise from bed, moving as if she were in front of the classroom, helping with homework, giving them an art lesson, leading a song. She taught at a bilingual elementary, so sometimes the instruction was in Spanish ("Niños, tienen que escuchar a la lectura, por favor. Mira, estoy tratando de explicar . . .") and other times in English ("One, two, three, all eyes on me!"), and there I was, wide awake in bed next to her, always unsure what to do. Eventually I learned to ignore her. I would just fall right back to sleep, leaving her to talk to the darkness. But this was harder to do when she was upset. I could tell in the tremor of her voice. Something had happened in her dream, a child had misbehaved, and she would rise from bed and hold out her arm and move her hand as though stroking the child's shoulder, or she would draw the child to her chest and pat the child's back. Then she would scold the child in the kindest and most patient of tones, and it would break my heart because I knew that she wanted nothing more than a child of her own and that I couldn't give her one. Instead, we had three cats, and we probably would've had more if I didn't put my foot down every time we saw a kitten.

When I saw the twins I wondered if she would've loved these children too. Of course she would've. She would have felt sorry for them. No mother to take care of them, and their father, Wayne, just a raving fat drunk whom I would see stomping around the yard, calling out their names while they hid from him. He was an imbecile, a fool. A man like him shouldn't have been allowed to have children. *He* could have children, but *I* couldn't?! I hated him for it. The only time I enjoyed the twins' mischief was when he was the target. They would construct pits for him to fall into; they would piss into his beer bottles and whiskey flask; they would spray him with water (it wasn't just me, thank goodness!); they would torture him as he lay in the grass nursing a hangover, tickling his nose with dandelions. And all he would do was holler. They would never listen, but still he hollered, and then he would chase after them, but he could never catch them; they were too fast, and they knew where to hide, or rather, Wayne didn't know how to look. "No, they're not in the tree!" I wanted to scream. Or, "You already looked underneath the car!" I watched it all from the Maestro's house, sipping coffee as I stared out the window, as though I were observing wild beasts at a zoo.

Once they had a party, and the father's friends came over, and maybe some older cousins because they resembled the twins, and they all sat in the weed lot and drank beer and whiskey straight from the bottle, and they yelled at each other

149

even though they were two feet away. Every other word was a cuss word. They called each other faggots and bitches and cunts and niggers; the women spoke like this too, and in their gravelly smoker voices the words sounded even more vulgar. Then someone pulled a switch from a tree and they started to play a game where one person would whip the other's back until he or she cried for mercy. They made horrible welts on each other's pasty skin, and all along the gathering cheered, and when blood was drawn they cheered louder. The entire time I kept glancing over at the twins, who sat on the porch step, and I saw them quiet, subdued even, a little lost in the mayhem. Together they shared a beer, trading sips. I saw one of the twins put his arm around his brother, and he kept it there, and then, shortly after, the other brother did the same. For that moment, these two shirtless, frail, dirty things, arms draped around each other, sipping a beer ten years before it was legal to do so, were a sight of beauty among that ugliness. Of course, it was quickly ruined. Someone saw them and called them fags, and then they were forced to play the whipping game. One brother whipped the other, and the gathering cheered them on, their father loudest of all, and the brother wielding the tree switch tried to smile, tried to muster the energy to whip harder, but I knew it pained him. I could see it in his face. But he kept at it until he drew blood, and while he was being cheered and offered a beer, his brother crumpled to the ground in tears. That was the first time I felt sorry for the twins. They never had a chance in this life.

I wasn't the only one in the neighborhood to call the cops on them. It seemed at least everyone had been the twins' victim at one point or another. Usually it followed the same course. If you couldn't prove they were the culprits, then not much could be done about it. So a few neighbors got cameras installed, but the twins never did the same misdeed twice—they were too inventive. You'd have to set up a camera in every corner of the yard and on every streetlamp in town in order to catch them. But they usually did themselves in anyway, like the time they stole a dirt bike and then crashed it. When the cops came they found one twin crying in the road, still tangled in the bike, and the other had left a trail of blood all the way back to his doorstep. Or when they broke into the elementary school and dumped a container of yellow tempera paint on the carpet and then stepped in the paint and left tracks of their shoes everywhere, two sets of shoe prints exactly the same size. The cops went directly to their door, asked to inspect the soles of their shoes, and then promptly arrested them. They were let go after a week.

I don't know what it was that finally got the bolder of the twins locked up in juvenile hall for an extended period of time. I just remember seeing the remaining twin slowly walk back and forth along the driveway, dejectedly, not knowing what to do with himself. One week passed, then two, then three, and still the lone twin just walked back and forth all day. He looked so sad and lonely that I started to feel bad for him. At one point, peering out from the guest-bedroom window, I saw him with a long stick, drawing or writing something in the dirt in front of the Maestro's house. He could've just been making marks, but he seemed far too concentrated on his task. Later I took a walk just to get out of the house, and on my return I remembered to look at what he had been doing. It was a drawing of some sorts. I looked closer and saw that it was a rendering of the Maestro's house. Actually, I thought it quite good considering it was made with a stick.

That night as I lay in bed I thought of the twin's drawing, and I thought of something my wife used to say: "There is wonder in each and every one of us." She would've said that if she saw his drawing. How had he learned to draw? I couldn't imagine him sitting inside that cramped apartment with enough time or space to make anything worthwhile, but somehow he had taught himself. Did the other twin know how to draw too? The next morning I awoke early and walked out to the studio. I hadn't yet been able to produce anything. I was too daunted by the Maestro's studio, by his lingering presence. I didn't want to mess anything up. But those were just excuses. The truth is

I felt no desire. But this morning was different. I felt inspired. I wanted to work, and I felt in a way that I owed it to the twin's drawing. Something about the marvel of its creation, that it was created at all, made me cherish my vocation, what talent I did have, what creativity I had in store. I had to find that spark again. So I entered the studio and pulled out a few sheets of paper, but as soon as the blank sheet was in front of me my inspiration turned to dread, and I could only think to myself, "What does it matter anymore?" I tried to muster the energy, but I gave up and walked outside. It was hot out and the sun felt good on my face. I walked around the Maestro's garden and picked up the hose to start watering, even though I'd watered the evening before and the Maestro had explicitly warned about overwatering. I didn't care, I just wanted a task.

Then I saw the twin. Through an archway on the side yard, just above the white picket fence, I saw him walking along the gravel driveway, forlorn as ever without his partner in crime. I was struck with an idea. I called out, "Hey! Hey!" He quickly raised his head from the ground and then looked as if he was about to take off before being scolded. "Wait!" I cried out, and I walked briskly toward him. He stood frozen.

"I saw your drawing yesterday!" I said, a little too excitedly. "The one that you did in the dirt."

He just looked at me with wide eyes. I knew he was quieter to begin with, but without his brother he was practically docile.

"It was of the Maestro's house," I said.

He looked up at me without recognition.

"I thought it was great," I continued. "Really great. I mean, you have talent."

Now he looked at me suspiciously. "What do you want?"

"Just that," I said. "I just wanted to let you know that I was impressed. I'm an artist too, just like the Maestro. Did you know he was an artist?"

He shrugged.

"Well, he's actually a famous artist. Well known, at least. He was my teacher long ago. Have you ever had lessons?"

"For what?"

"Drawing lessons."

He shook his head.

"Would you like some?" I asked, surprising myself. I wasn't sure I wanted to offer, but wasn't that why I had approached him in the first place?

"I hate school," he said

"This wouldn't be like school. We'd just draw, that's it. The Maestro has plenty of paper and drawing supplies in the studio."

He shook his head unsurely. I could tell he was thinking about it.

"Let me know if you change your mind," I said.

He walked away without saying a word, and in a way I was relieved. "At least I tried," I told my wife.

The next day I saw him again, walking the same path along the potholed driveway. He wore a sweat shirt with the hood pulled tightly over his head. I was standing in the window, sipping my coffee. It was early in the morning, just before seven o'clock, and I wondered why he wasn't still in bed or at least in his apartment. I thought maybe he woke up and couldn't stand to be alone in the same cramped room as his father, whom I imagined snored very loudly. When I finished my coffee I walked outside to water the daisies on the side yard. The twin walked by again with his hands dug deep in his pockets. I nodded my head and he looked up at me sheepishly before glancing away. Ten minutes later he walked by again, slower this time, and even though he didn't look in my direction I felt as though he wanted me to address him.

"Up early this morning," I said.

Without looking up he nodded and continued walking by.

"Mornings are a good time for drawing," I said. Actually, for me this wasn't the case; I preferred to read or take care of tasks, but it was something to say.

He stopped abruptly and looked up at me.

"Why?" he asked.

"Why?" I said. "Well . . ." I chuckled, a little embarrassed. "They just are. Good light to draw by, I guess."

He seemed to accept this.

"Would you like to give it a shot?" I asked.

He shook his head and ran off, leaving me to wonder if I'd said something weird.

That afternoon I was in the Maestro's studio, staring at a blank sheet of paper, holding a piece of charcoal in my right hand, feeling the same sick-to-my-stomach sensation and asking myself, "What does it even matter anymore?" when I heard a loud knock on the studio door. As I opened it I had a feeling it was going to be the twin.

It wasn't. It was his father, Wayne. He stood there with a tank top so threadbare that I could see the pink of his oblong nipples and the dark hairy pit of his belly button. He was wearing jean shorts and camel-colored work boots with orange soles. He looked like he hadn't showered, shaved, or slept in days. Even from a distance of a few feet I could smell his body odor and the stench of whiskey.

"Can I help you?" I asked, realizing we had never spoken.

"My name is Wayne," he said, "and my boy tells me you're offering drawing lessons. I'd like to participate, if that's all right with you."

I almost laughed out loud. "I—I—well, I—don't know. You want drawing lessons? I was offering them to your son—"

"He can't draw worth shit. Don't waste your time on him."

Now I did start to laugh. "Well, from what I saw, your son actually draws quite well for his age."

"That's horseshit! I can almost guarantee that he took one of my drawings to show you."

"No, you're mistaken. I personally saw him drawing."

Wayne starting to run his fingers through his long, stringy hair, and then he began pulling at it so that greasy clumps stood on end. His voice became whinier. "You're just like the old man, you know that? You're just like him. You don't know talent when you see it. My boy can't draw! He won't even listen to your lessons. You'll just be wasting your time!"

154

I didn't know what to say. I was dumb struck. I couldn't even imagine an interaction between the Maestro and Wayne, let alone one that involved artistic merit.

"Well," I finally managed, "I should really get back to my work. I'm sorry, but I'm very busy."

"That's what he always said too!" Wayne cried before turning around and storming off. There was an apple hanging low on the tree, and he swatted it as he walked by.

The following day, my work (or lack thereof) was disrupted when I again heard a knock on the studio door. I hesitated, worrying it would be Wayne, but the knock was different this time, more delicate. Wayne's knock had sounded more like he had banged the door with an open palm.

"Who is it?" I asked.

No one answered. I slowly opened the door and found the twin. I breathed a sigh of relief. He was standing there shirtless, his arms behind his back, his blue eyes looking up at me nervously. He looked like a startled cat. His mouth was bright red, as though he'd just had some fruit punch.

"You came!" I said. "Come on in!"

He took a cautious step into the studio, looking around himself, his eyes darting every which way as he absorbed the new surroundings. Momentarily relieved of my own creative block, I reached for the sheet of paper I had been staring at for the previous hour and said, "I had this waiting for you!" I pulled up a stool and patted it. "Take a seat! I'll get you some drawing utensils, how about that?"

I felt as if I was shouting. He still hadn't said a word. I found him a piece of charcoal, a shading stub, and an eraser. I got my own as well and told him that we'd both draw together. I pulled out another sheet of paper for myself and clipped it to a drawing board. Then we sat, neither of us making a move to place the charcoal to paper. An awkward silence reigned in the studio, and for a moment I thought of rising to turn on the radio, but I didn't feel like fiddling for a new station. I was sure he wouldn't want to listen to whatever talk show was currently on NPR.

"What do you want me to draw?" he said finally.

"I don't know," I said.

"What are you going to draw?"

I shook my head and laughed. "That's a good question. What do you usually like to draw?"

"When I'm with my brother we like to draw zombies eating people."

"Oh, is that right?" I said, imagining the Maestro's five-dollar sheets of paper covered in gory zombie drawings. "How about when you're alone, what do you like to draw?"

He shrugged.

"Well," I said, "What if we drew each other?"

"What do you mean?"

"While I'm drawing you, you can draw me. How does that sound?"

He seemed to like this idea, and we set to work at once. At first I felt somewhat uneasy, drawing this young shirtless boy, and I almost wished for the sake of appearances that I'd suggested something else. But soon I became engrossed in my subject, and I lost myself in the details of his face, his bony frame, and his eyes so focused on his own drawing. At one point I asked him what his name was, and without looking up from his task he mumbled, "Nicholas." I told him my name, but he didn't seem to care. In fact, the entire time he was drawing he barely glanced up at me, which is a mistake beginners make—they forget to see their subject and rely too heavily on what they *think* they see—and so I told him this. "Observation," I said, "careful studying is the key to good drawings." He didn't even flinch. He just kept focused on his task, his mouth pursed in concentration. At some point I stopped, but he continued for a good while longer before stopping too. "You done?" I asked. He nodded. I looked at my own drawing. I felt a great weight off my chest. I had placed charcoal to paper for the first time in months. The boy was a worthy subject. I held it up for him to see. I thought he would be impressed by the likeness, but he just looked at it as if he'd seen a thousand portraits of himself.

"Can I see your drawing?" I asked, rising to look over his shoulder. "It's of me, right?"

"Yup," he said.

I leaned closer. He had drawn me all right—to make it clear he'd written the word "you" and an arrow—along with a zombie eating out my brains.

The drawing sessions continued. Every afternoon he would show up and we would draw each other; or I would draw him and he would draw either zombies eating me or me as a zombie. To be honest, he didn't have much talent. I started to wonder if he was even the one who drew the Maestro's house in the dirt. Maybe someone else had drawn it and he was just making marks around it. He did seem to enjoy drawing, at least, which was good. Of course, he didn't listen at all to my advice or pointers, but I figured that he was benefiting simply by drawing every day. I know that I was. Before, I couldn't stay in the studio, but now I had a reason to be there. I had a subject to work from, and when I viewed my drawings all together I thought I was really on to something. I wasn't sure what, but it felt different. Nicholas had an aura about him; a tension where vulnerability met dogged determination. He was alone in this world, and yet he had survived, or he and his brother—whose name I learned was Dennis—had survived, and this was admirable. They were fighters. Just very misdirected fighters. If they could channel their energy and imagination and fearlessness into something other than trouble, they would be okay. If not, that same combination would land them in prison. I even started to feel that maybe I could play a role in ensuring that the twins found the right path. I imagined my wife smiling down on me. This is what she would've done, I thought.

One day Nicholas was a little later than usual, but I soon heard a knock on the studio door and I rushed to open it, quickly turning back to my task without checking to see who was there. I just assumed it was Nicholas. "Your paper is already out," I said. "I was expecting you an hour ago."

"My dad wouldn't let me come until now," he said.

"Not a problem, as long as you came. Shall we get started?" I sat down with my sheet of paper and grabbed a china marker. I had planned on trying a different technique that day.

"Okay, I'm ready to start drawing," he said as he plopped down in his seat and picked up a piece of charcoal. "Hmmmmmm, what should I draw?"

I furrowed my brow. Usually Nicholas wasn't this talkative. He just came in and set right to work. I didn't think much of it, though, as I was anxious to start drawing. I picked up the china marker and unwrapped the paper to reveal more of the grease tip. I stared at the contours of Nicholas's torso, shirtless as always, and made a few measurements. I lightly traced up to his neck, his jawbone, his ear, and then fixed a spot on top of his head. I was making a full-body portrait, so I hadn't yet reached the face, but already I noticed that Nicholas was more fidgety than usual. I glanced up and saw that he wasn't focused on his drawing either. He usually made strong committed lines, pressing hard on the paper, but today he was scribbling rapidly, looking at me and then back at the paper, jumping from one end to the other. I thought this strange, but wasn't I also experimenting that day? I continued to lightly shade in some of the volumes when he moved his pose completely. "You'll have to sit still," I said, without looking up.

"You like drawing me a lot, huh?" he asked.

"Yes, sure," I said absently.

Then after a pause, he asked, "Would you like to draw me in a different way?"

"Well, I'm trying this china marker. Maybe you'd like to try a different drawing utensil too. I can take a look. Let me just get down your pose first."

"I meant would you like to draw me differently?"

"What do you mean?" I asked, still only half listening. I made the final measurement and looked up.

"What if I took off my pants?" he asked. "Would you like to draw me then?"

"What the—" I stopped. It took me only a brief moment to realize that I wasn't talking to Nicholas. They may have been identical to the untrained eye—even to the inattentive eye—but now that I was looking at him the differences were vast. He didn't have Nicholas's scar on his lip or the one on his chin; he was paler and had fewer freckles, probably because he'd been locked up for the month; his hairline was lower; his ears stuck out more; his overall facial structure was wider. These were all very slight things, but taken together they made all the difference. It wasn't just the physical differences though. There was something else about him. I looked into his eyes and had the strange sensation that there was nothing behind them.

"You're Dennis," I said.

"What are you talking about?"

"Where's Nicholas?" I asked.

"I'm Nicholas."

"You're not fooling me," I said. "I know you're Dennis, and you tried to play a little trick on me. Well, very funny. Now, where's your brother?"

Dennis began to cackle. "Don't you want to see my drawing of you?" he asked, obviously not caring that I'd caught on to his game. He held the paper up for me to see. I didn't even look at the drawing. I set my drawing board aside and rose from my chair. I very briskly walked to the studio door and opened it. I turned to Dennis and said, "You need to leave," and I pointed outside.

He was smiling as if he was enjoying himself thoroughly. He rose from his seat and sauntered toward me, passing his hand along a table and knocking over everything on it—an empty coffee mug, a plastic container full of colored pencils, a stack of books, an empty Coke can—smiling all the while as though he had a secret he couldn't bear to keep to himself.

"Hurry up," I said sternly.

He walked by and stood at the threshold of the door. "My brother told me what you did to him," he said.

"What are you talking about?"

He shook his head in exaggerated disapproval. "How you touched him. He told me all about it."

"Get out of here!" I exclaimed, and instinctively I reached out to nudge him from the doorway so that I could close the door. Immediately, he turned rabid. "Don't fucking touch me!" he screamed, his face beet red. "Don't ever fucking touch me or I'll fucking kill you. I'll fucking kill you!"

"Get out of here!" I cried again. He moved just enough for me to slam the door shut. My heart was pounding. I couldn't think straight. I didn't know whether to stand or sit. I sure as hell wasn't going to resume drawing. I took the one I had started and crumpled it up into my hands and tossed it into the wastebasket. It was then that I heard a large thud against the door. I rushed toward it, then hesitated, not knowing what I would find on the other side. Maybe I'd open it and be assailed by rocks or dirt clods. I waited for a moment and nudged open the door slowly. I peeked my head out. I looked around for the twin, and in the distance, through low-hanging tree branches and leaves, I saw both twins running down the driveway. My heart sank. Nicholas had played a part in this. I looked down and saw what had created the thud. It was a large terra-cotta pot, now in pieces. It would've been too large for one person to lift alone. The plant had fallen out, its roots poking through clumps of wet dirt.

"Fucking kids," I muttered to myself. My heart was still beating fast, my hands trembling. I wasn't so much angry as deeply unsettled. I wanted to excuse Nicholas somehow. Maybe he didn't know what his brother was going to do. Maybe Dennis had exerted his power over his brother, and Nicholas had no choice but to play along. But hadn't he helped his brother hurl the pot against the door? I recalled when Dennis had sprayed me with the hose and they'd both laughed at me. I had wanted revenge. I didn't want revenge anymore. I just wanted the twins to disappear. I didn't want to see them ever again, and I felt myself a fool for thinking that I could change the direction of their miserable existence. I found all the drawings I'd made in the past month, all of them of Nicholas drawing, Nicholas focused and attentive, Nicholas lost in the world of his zombie-filled imagination, and I crumpled them up and tossed them in the trash.

I heard another knock. I didn't want to answer it. I wanted it to be a figment of my imagination. But the knock came again and again, and I briefly entertained the idea that it was Nicholas returning to apologize. I rose from the chair and walked in a daze toward the studio door. I opened it to find Wayne. He was standing there holding a white binder and looking down at the broken pot.

"Wayne, I can't," I said. My voice was weak almost to the point of breaking. "I can't."

"I told you my boys were worthless," he said, as he lightly brushed soil and broken pieces of terra-cotta off the step with his boot. "They don't listen to anybody. They don't listen to me, they won't listen to you. They—"

"Wayne, stop. Please. I don't want to hear any apologies."

"Hell, I didn't come to apologize. I already warned you about them. Look, I'll come right out with it. I don't want to take up any more of your time. I just wanted you to see for yourself what I'm capable of doing. I think that if you and me worked together, I might be able to do something with the talent God gave me. Now, I'm just going to leave this here for you to look at when you get a chance, okay?"

He placed the binder in my hands, forcing me to hold it or else let it fall. He quickly turned and walked away, almost skipping as he reached around to hike up his sagging jean shorts. "Wayne," I called out limply, but he was already on the other side of the yard. I stared at the white binder in my hands. It was dingy and worn. Curiosity compelled me to open it. Every page was protected in a plastic slip sheet. On the first page was a quote by Edmund Burke: "The only thing necessary for the triumph of evil is for good men to do nothing." After that I found pages of awkwardly rendered copies of comic-book heroes repeating more or less the same thing. Captain America: "If we don't do anything then evil will triumph over good." Spider-Man: "Evil will not triumph over good as long as we fight against it!" Batman having a conversation with the Green Lantern: "It doesn't matter if we're good. If we don't do anything then evil will triumph."

I closed the binder and pressed it to my chest. I didn't know what to feel at that moment. I just knew that I didn't want that binder in my possession a minute longer. I had to rid myself of it. I walked out of the studio and practically ran through the Maestro's garden. After struggling to open the warped and sagging side gate, I entered the neighboring complex and walked down the potholed driveway toward Wayne and the twins' apartment. Once on the porch I knocked on the door and looked around myself. I could hear the hum and hollow drip of the swamp cooler. I smelled cigarette smoke and cat shit. I saw broken glass everywhere. I saw a checkerboard on top of a dirty Styrofoam ice chest, the black and red plastic pieces scattered everywhere. No one came to the door. I knocked louder, this time with my palm open, slapping my hand against the doorframe until my skin stung. I stopped and looked to my left, and that was when I found myself, for the first time, staring at the Maestro's beautiful home as if I were his neighbor. As if I weren't house-sitting; as if I didn't know the Maestro at all; as if I'd entered some alternate reality where I was doomed to live alone in this squalid one-bedroom apartment with my incorrigible offspring, drawing nothing but comic-book characters battling evil for the rest of my life. I imagined stepping outside, day after day, forced to contemplate the mirage next door. For that's what the Maestro's house looked like: an illusion never to be touched.

"Good God," I said to myself. I placed the binder on the doorstep and hurried back to the Maestro's yard as quickly as I could.

Several days passed before I was able to muster the energy to return to the studio. "You have to work," I kept telling myself. But when I finally entered I merely sat down on the Maestro's comfy old paint-splattered chair, leaned my head back, and stared at the ceiling. I charted the cobwebs gathering in the corners. I followed the slow rotation of the ceiling fans. I searched for faces and animals in the ceiling texture as though I were looking at cloud formations. I did this until my neck began to hurt. As I was massaging the kink out, I happened to turn my head toward Dennis's drawing, which was still on the drawing board where he'd last left it. Somehow I wasn't surprised to find my countenance staring back at me. A mess of quick lines, nothing more than raw gestural marks, and that little bastard had conjured up the wretchedness of my life. I picked up the drawing and stared at it, unable to turn away. In the back of my mind I could hear my wife laughing, the delightful mocking laugh she made when she was proved right about something. I started to laugh with her, because what else can one do?

The Stuttering Roommate

—◊—

A LOT OF people feel sorry for those who stutter. Not me. I once lived with a stutterer, and the son of a bitch drove me crazy. Now already you probably think I'm the true son of a bitch in the situation, and that just goes to show you that most people feel sorry for stutterers without listening to the facts.

His name was Manolo and we lived together in the Wayside Apartments over there in Knights Landing. If you've ever been to Knights Landing and seen the Wayside, you know it's a shit hole, even if they do repaint it every couple of years. Paint or no paint, you can't cover up mold, rotted wood, and rat carcasses in the insulation. I shared a place with five others. I considered them nice guys, but they fall into the category described above: they all felt sorry for Manolo and catered to his every whim. We worked in the tomato fields and the peach orchards in the summer, did construction work in the fall, and in the winter if you didn't head back home you'd wash dishes.

The first time I met Manolo he just shook my hand and stayed quiet, which I thought admirable. When you have to live with five other guys in an apartment the size of your last crap, it's best that a few of them are quiet and mind their own business. Well, evening time came around, and the silent new guy finally opened his mouth. "Wha-wha-whas f-f-for d-ih-nn-er?" he said. I just about pissed my pants I laughed so hard. I couldn't catch my breath for five minutes straight! Then I realized no one else was laughing. I turned to the other guys and said, "What the hell is going on with him?" Pedro, one of the roommates, ignored me and said to Manolo, "We're going to have tacos al pastor, how does that sound?" Manolo looked ready to cry. He stammered, "D-d-a-t see-see-seems o-o-oh-okay, bu-bu-bu-bu-but-but I-I-I-I'd rather ha-ha-ha-have po-po-po-po-po-po-posole." Posole! I would have laughed again if it weren't for his outlandish request. Since when does the new guy choose what we have for dinner? I was in the place five years before I got to make requests just for breakfast, and he was already writing up a menu! But my roommates agreed. Posole it was. Pedro, Marcos, and Rigoberto were leaving to the Plug'n'Jug Market to pick up fixings, and they told me to come along. I told them I didn't want to, but they insisted.

On the way they scolded me. "We can't believe you!" they cried. "Don't you see he has a speech problem?" "Can't you understand that he's ashamed of his affliction, and here you go and laugh in his face!" "He's here in the country just two weeks, and already you have to make him feel horrible!" "You should be ashamed of yourself!" "Put yourself in his shoes!" I couldn't get a word in with these asses upbraiding me for doing what God gave me the gift to do: laugh when I found something funny. They finally finished and I said to them, "Come on, guys, admit it: didn't he sound like Elias's donkey of a car with the put-put-put-tatta-tat engine!" And the hypocrites all laughed until they were red in the face. They laughed even harder when I mimicked the dinner request. "You sound just like him!" they said. I probably did; I've always liked acting.

Well, we returned home and I promised myself I wasn't going to react when this guy started talking again, but there we were cooking up his damn posole while he remained in the bedroom watching television. Finally, I said, "He requests posole and we have to cook it without him lifting a finger?" Girolamo, the one who invited Manolo to live with us, said, "Television helps him enunciate the words because they talk more clearly." I just about fell over. I called out, "New guy,

166

everybody works no matter if you're retarded or not. How's that for enunciation!" You would've thought I'd called his mother a slut for his reaction. He appeared in the kitchen all purple in the face, tears streaming down his cheeks, and said, "I I I I ah-ah-am no-no-not a a a re-re-retard!" And then my roommates jumped on my case again, telling me I was a no-good lowlife, and didn't I know better than to call somebody a retard, and all these other things to make me feel as if I were the worst person on earth. Well, maybe I am, maybe I'm not; all I know is Manolo got his posole and watched his cop-chase show while I prepared the ham hock. Enunciation!

So that's how it was for a long while. The stuttering bastard got all he wanted. He picked what we watched on television, selected all our meals, decided whether we'd go for a stroll in either the Woodland mall or the one in Sacramento, never had to pay for gas, never was asked to chip in for beer, all because as soon as he uttered so much as a "he-he-hell-lo" the room grew silent, everyone's good humor disappeared, and a solemn mood came over the gathering, as if no one had ever heard a man struggle to say hello before. I didn't let it bother me. I just tried to make light of it, which seemed to make enemies of the rest of my roommates. "Come on," I told them, "you guys act like he's dying of cancer, for God's sake!" They told me that Manolo had been beaten as a child and was made fun of by the neighborhood kids. I said, "Who wasn't?" They said that his own mother had brought him to a curandera to sear his tongue with a burning rod. I said, "Tough love never hurt anybody!" They told me that he'd been picked on all his life, and the least they could do was be understanding. I told them there was a word for men who like other men too much.

Then there was the time we went to the county fair, and, while trying to distract Pedro as he played a dart-balloon game, I accidentally dropped my corn dog on this cholo's shoe. The hothead was ready to take the matter to the next level, and so was I, but guess who came to the rescue, saying, "He-he-he-hey don-don't f-f-figh-fight, we we j-j-just try-trying to to to wi-wi-win a stuh-stuh-stuh-stuhf-stuhfed beh-beh-bear." Apparently hoodlums also have soft spots for stutterers, because the cholo nodded his head and let the matter drop, ketchup on his shoe and all. Of course, everyone congratulated Manolo on his composure and peace-keeping skills. For my part, I asked him if "winning a stuffed bear" was really the best he could think of.

"It saved your ass," Girolamo said.

"Come again?" I asked.

"It kept you from getting your ass beat."

"You mean he kept *me* from beating that cholo's ass."

Everyone laughed, but I was serious—I have no tolerance for instigators. For the rest of the evening Manolo walked around like the official keeper of the peace. When they told the story later they liked to say I was scared shitless, and thanks to Manolo I'm still alive today, and if it hadn't been for Manolo's quick thinking they'd have had to drop me off at the hospital, and other such nonsense in order to make Manolo feel better about his lot in life.

But the following event is what really turned me against stutterers and all those who cater to their every whim. Every weekday night La Que Buena radio station has a show called *Operation Cupid*. Listeners are invited to call in and leave their phone numbers with the hope that some girl out there will like the sound of their voice and give them a call. Always seemed like a pathetic way of meeting ladies, but I'm old-fashioned like that. The DJ has a deep baritone voice made for shows like this. I don't hesitate to say he's possibly the smoothest guy I've ever met, or listened to, I guess, because I've never actually met him. I also have to admit that I've called in a few times myself, but just to request songs and give a shout-out to all my people from Michoacán. Anyway, Manolo wasn't a bad-looking guy: tall, good strong jawbone. Every time we'd go to a dance in Woodland, either at La Fogata or La Finca de Rivera, some girls would eye him, and he'd have Pedro or Girolamo go ask them to dance for him. The girls would be into him too, but as soon as the dancing was over he'd start talking, stammering and stuttering and making a fool of himself, and they'd think the guy was drunk off his ass. I'd explain to the ladies that he wasn't drunk at all, in fact he hardly ever drank, he just had problems talking. "So he always talks like that?" they'd ask. "Yup," I'd say. I'm an honest guy; who am I to lead ladies astray? Manolo would be discouraged, and all our roommates of course would tell him not to worry, that the right girl was out there, and that if a girl had a problem with stutterers she was bound to be bad news when it came to marriage and raising children. They even told him that after a while they hardly even noticed his stuttering, which couldn't have been farther from the truth, but they belong to the sort that thinks dishonesty makes life more bearable.

So one day I'm sitting out in front of my compadre Chuy's trailer, which is on the far side of the Wayside, and Pedro, Girolamo, Marcos, and Rigoberto have joined me for a few beers. Manolo told us he was going to take a nap so we let him be. Chuy had his radio playing, and we were talking a whole bunch of nonsense about women and making money and returning home to Michoacán someday and buying houses the size of soccer fields, when *Operation Cupid* starts and we all quiet to listen. We heard a few listeners call in, and then I initiated a game called "Pansy or not," a very simple game requiring participants to either say "Pansy" or "Not a pansy." Most of us called the callers pansies, but when Pedro spoke too soon and said, "Not a pansy," I called out, "You're a pansy for thinking he's not a pansy!" Then no one wanted to play the game, because they accused me of always looking for ways to question their manhood. So what? Such is life, one long proof of how big your balls are. At least that's what my father told me, may God rest his soul and forgive his many indiscretions.

Well, we kind of lost interest in the radio show and had started talking about other subjects when Girolamo, who was sitting closest to the radio, cried, "Shhhhh, it's Manolo!" He turned up the volume and we listened. Sure enough, it was our stuttering roommate!

"What does he think he's doing?" I exclaimed, laughing. Everyone shushed me.

"Compadre, what can I do for you tonight?" the DJ asked.

There was a pause on the line. The DJ said, "Compadre, are you there?"

I cried, "Oh shit, what's Manolo doing—he's asking for it!"

I was shushed again.

Manolo started in, "I I I ju-ju-just wou-would-would lie-lie-lie-lie-lie-like to—"

The DJ cut him off, "You would like to leave your number for some beautiful lady out there, isn't that right, compadre?"

Manolo stammered a yes.

The DJ must have caught on that this caller wasn't the usual nervous pre-ejaculator, because instead of asking Manolo where he was from, the DJ made a guess: "You sound like a countryman from Michoacán, am I right?" All Manolo had to say was yes, but he decided to make things difficult. He found it necessary to state the exact little town he hailed from: "Pa-pa-pa-pata-mo-mo-moro-moroso." "Very good," the DJ responded, pausing to collect his thoughts, probably not sure what the hell had just been said. Then, still trying to make the phone call less difficult for all involved, he asked, "And how about where you're located now? Let me guess, Sacramento?" This time he wasn't so lucky. Manolo stammered no.

"Roseville?"

"No-no."

"Lincoln?"

"Nnnn-o."

"Stockton?"

"N-n-no-no."

"Modesto?"

"N-n-n-n-o."

"Vacaville?"

"N-n-n-no-no."

"Dixon?"

"N-n-n-no-no."

"Woodland?"

"N-n-no-no."

The DJ sighed and chuckled gently. "Well then, compadre,

it's not important where you're from. The ladies know you're in the area and—"

Manolo cut him off. "I-I-I-I'm fr-fra-fra-from Wi-Wi-Wi-Winters."

"Winters!" I cried out. "That's Manolo from Knights Landing if I've ever heard him. Does he think we won't know it's him?! Ha!" This time no one shushed me. Everyone was quiet. I looked around at my previously jovial beer-drinking buddies. Like always, Manolo had put everyone in a shitty mood.

The phone call ended, the DJ moved on to other callers, and we were left wondering how to approach Manolo about his *Operation Cupid* debut. I suggested we call him from a pay phone and pretend we're expectant ladies, appreciative of his courage and valor in the face of such obstacles. Pedro called me a son of a bitch. Rigoberto told me that if I said anything about the phone call he'd personally kick my ass. I told him he might as well kick my ass right now, because not saying anything about the phone call was like busying about the kitchen while your wife fucks your best friend in the bedroom. My comment was received with a few blank stares. I tried again: "Ignoring the phone call is like sweeping around an elephant in the middle of the room!" Rigoberto told me to keep my mouth shut for once in my life.

They left me to my beers.

An hour later I decided I'd had enough and headed back to the apartment. I resolved to keep quiet about the phone call as much as was possible. I entered the apartment and found Manolo sitting on his bed and staring at the phone on his bedside table. He didn't even look up when I entered. I changed my clothes and brushed my teeth. Out in the room Manolo was still staring at the phone. I figured it couldn't hurt to ask him what he was doing. Pedro and Rigoberto, who were lying in bed, shot me icy stares. Manolo told me, "I I I I ah-ah-am wa-wa-way-way-waiting for a a a pho-phone call." I told him very well and got into bed.

I don't know why, but at that moment I started thinking about my last girlfriend and all the times I had waited for her

171

phone calls. Just as I would be about to lose my mind she'd call, always apologetic, telling me that it wasn't her fault, that she'd been held up with her friends, her family, or whatever excuse she invented. I'd forgive her, and then sure enough she'd do it again the next time. One day she just never called me back. Remembering this put me in a foul mood, and I was suddenly resentful of Manolo for reminding me of old memories I thought had been dealt with and forgotten. I looked over at him and said, "Manolo, staring at the phone doesn't make it ring, take it from one who knows."

My roommates all shot me looks of disgust. Rigoberto was ready to pounce on me.

Manolo replied, "I I I I knnn-know, b-b-b-bu-but, I I I ju-ju-just wan-want to." I rolled my eyes. The radio was on and I could hear that *Operation Cupid* was wrapping up. I brought it to Manolo's attention. "Look at that, the evening hours pass by so quickly. *Operation Cupid* is already over."

I saw Manolo's shoulders slump and I felt guilty. I made amends with a little fib. "You know, I bet those ladies out there just keep calling until all hours of the morning. I bet it takes them a while to work up the nerve. Hell, my cousin called in once and this girl called him at three in the morning."

Rigoberto told me to shut up.

"I didn't say anything!" I said. "I was just commenting on the fact."

He told me to go to bed. Normally I would have told him to go stick it where it was unnatural, but the beers had made me tired so I decided to shut off my lamp and try to sleep. I nodded off, but I woke with a start what felt like hours later. I looked at the clock. It had only been a half hour. The room was dark except for the lamp on the far side of the room. Manolo was still there on his bed, staring at the phone. I was about to ask him if he wouldn't mind shutting off his lamp when I heard a sniffling noise. I looked over at Pedro and saw him with his head buried into his pillow.

"Pedro?" I whispered.

Pedro looked up at me. His eyes sparkled. The son of a bitch was crying. "What do you want?" he asked.

"Are you crying?" I whispered.

"What the fuck does it look like I'm doing?"

"What are you crying for?"

He told me to leave him alone. What was happening to my roommates? I turned to the wall and tried to fall back to sleep, but I could still hear Pedro's sniffling. I grew angry at Manolo sitting over there like an idiot, making everyone, including me, feel bad about his predicament. I rose in bed and told him, "No one's going to call, damn it." He didn't answer me, so I repeated myself. He looked up and said, "Suh-suh-suhmone will, may-may-maybe."

I told him to go to bed. "If the phone rings you'll wake up."

He said, "Le-le-let me be, ju-jus-just le-le-let me be."

I let him be. Finally he shut off the lamp, and I thought the ordeal was over. Maybe tomorrow we could laugh about it. But several moments later I heard strange yelps coming from his side of the room, yelps shrill and violent. The next few yelps were muffled, then they grew louder, then muffled again, followed by yelps louder and more pained. Then they turned into sobs. I switched on my lamp. "What's going on over there?" I cried. Manolo was beside himself. He was laid out on the bed, his arms extended like Christ on the Cross, his body convulsing.

"Goddamn it!" I yelled at him. "Get a hold of yourself! What did you think would happen if you called in to a radio show? Did you think God would intervene and take away your stutter?"

My other roommates switched on their lamps.

"I-I-I-I'm so lo-lo-lone-lonely," he said through blubbered sobs.

"You're lonely?" I cried. "You're lonely? We're six men in a bedroom that stinks like the sweat of our asses! It doesn't get worse than this! But why do you have to make us feel bad along with you? Tonight you make Pedro cry, and you make me remember my ex-girlfriend, who didn't have the decency to call me back even though I said, 'I'll hear from you on Thursday?' and she said, 'Yes, on Thursday.' Well many Thursdays have passed and still no phone call! Don't you understand that you're not the only one suffering here?"

"I-I-I'm sah-sah-soh-soh-sorry!" he cried.

"Sorry? No, it's too late for sorry. No, no, no! When I left Michoacán she was *my* girl, she told me she would wait forever for my return, and I told her I'd cross mountains, rivers, and valleys to see her! And the heartless bitch didn't call me back! And I had forgotten all about it until tonight, with you and your request-line call and your waiting and your pitiful sobs. Goddamn it, don't you understand? I was you not too long ago . . . Hell, it's only been a few years! I sat there on the bed, watching the phone, waiting and waiting and waiting, but that's just life—you move on, you sack up, you—you—you—you—see, now you have me stuttering like an ass!"

"I'm I'm sor-sor-sor—"

"It's too late for sorries!" I yelled at him.

Pedro and Rigoberto told me to calm down.

"Calm down? I am calm! I'm as calm as can be considering the circumstances!"

Pedro told me I was overreacting.

"Overreacting? You're the one weeping into your pillow like a little girl with socks hiked to your knees!"

He told me to shut up or he'd sock me in my nose. I told him he'd better get in a punch first before I unleashed on him a hundred blows worthy of God's vengeful wrath. That was when he reached across the bed and slapped me across the cheek. Surprised, it took me a moment before I leaped from my bed to his bed and began pummeling his liver just like my favorite boxer Daniel Ponce de León. Soon, Rigoberto, Marcos, and Girolamo were on my back, pulling me off him. I swung at them too, blind with rage. Pedro must have gotten an elbow to my nose, because my eyes stung like hell.

I finally gave up the fight. Too many against one. I collapsed on the floor, my eyes stinging with tears from the sucker punch.

"Fight me one-on-one," I yelled. They didn't answer me. "At least Manolo has quit his crying," I said.

"You're the only one who's crying now," Girolamo told me.

"I'm not crying! Pedro got in a cheap shot to my nose."

"Look at you," Rigoberto said, "giving everyone shit about being a pansy, and you're the one crying over a girl who dumped you years ago."

Once again I insisted I wasn't crying, that I had just been hit in the nose.

"You can't even admit to crying," Pedro said.

"It's my nose!" I yelled.

Then the phone rang. Everyone grew quiet and Manolo's eyes grew wide. "Pick it up," Pedro told him.

"Do do do you think think I I I should?"

My assailants all nodded, hopeful smiles creeping onto their faces.

Manolo picked up. "He-he-hell-hello?"

Looking back, I wish that it had been a girl. Instead it was a couple of drunks who jotted down Manolo's number with the hopes of having some fun. I can picture the situation: they must have gotten distracted, forgot about the stuttering caller, drank some more, then came across the number hours later, saving me from my roommates who weren't aware that getting hit in the nose was like chopping an onion. When Manolo hung up the phone and told us what had happened, I thought it was a good joke. Still, I shouldn't have laughed. But I did, and that sealed my fate! The next day Rigoberto and Girolamo told me that I should find another place to live.

I ended up moving to Woodland and fell in with another group of guys. I told them about Manolo and how he had used his affliction to milk my ex-roommates of their manhood. I told them about the phone call too. I thought at the very least they would get a chuckle, but they were as humorless as everyone else. They stared into their beers, sullen as can be, as though I had informed each one of them that both their parents had died and that the girl they had left behind in La Piedad was now shacking up with their brother. Exasperated, I stopped and asked, "Why do you feel sorry for *him*? You don't even know the guy!" And they just shook their heads and shrugged their shoulders, and two of them removed their hats and scratched their heads, and one spoke for all the rest when he mumbled, "Good God, man, the poor guy stutters," as if that was all that needed to be said.

Cesar Trejo's Knuckles

—⟋⟍⟍—

I

I DO DRYWALL. I do any kind of construction, really, but technically I do drywall because I'm a member of the Local 9109, the drywallers union (meaning just drywall, as opposed to the tapers). But I do a lot of side jobs too, under-the-table stuff. It was on one of these side jobs that I became an investigator. I just call it that because I don't have any other name for it. In my mind, you see, there was a mystery, something I couldn't understand, and I had to get to the bottom of it. It started when my friend Julio, who owns Zitios Bar, called and told me that some drunk had put a hole in the bathroom wall. Could I fix it? Of course, I told him. So I went over to Zitios, inspected the damage, and gave him a good estimate. Then we had a beer and talked about our upcoming fantasy-football draft picks. That weekend I patched the hole, mudded and sanded it, and then painted it. You couldn't even tell there had been a hole.

A few weeks went by, and Julio called again to tell me that some jackass had punched several holes in the wall. Could I come back? Of course, I told him. This time, though, I didn't think it was just one person punching the holes in the wall. "What do you mean? How can you tell?" Julio asked. I told him that I didn't know for sure, I just couldn't imagine someone's fist standing up to the impact. "There'd have to be a little blood somewhere. Maybe the guy's fist is made of steel," I said, "but his skin can't be." Julio nodded, but he didn't seem to care if it was one guy or ten, he just wanted it fixed. So I fixed it, taking extra care to make sure the seams didn't show. I was thinking that if you wanted to punch a hole in the wall, then you're probably looking to punch through a patch rather than the drywall itself. But then I thought if you're drunk you're really not paying attention to anything. I was just wasting my time.

A few weeks later, Julio asked me to come by Zitios again. I showed up on Friday afternoon, and this time there were just two holes, but one of them looked like a boot had made it rather than a fist. "Look," Julio told me, "is there anything you can do to reinforce the wall? I'm getting tired of this happening." I told him I could get thicker drywall, but unless I did the whole wall there'd be a slope. I could even it out as best as I could, but there'd still be a slope. He told me, "It's the bathroom at a bar, man, I couldn't give a shit. I just don't want any more holes." So I put in the thicker ⅝" drywall, taped and mudded it, sanded it, and then painted it, and all the while that I was painting it I kept wondering to myself if other bars in town had this same problem. I could make a business out of it. Offer double-reinforced walls for bathrooms. I got so excited about the idea that right after finishing I went to Kenny's Bar a few blocks over and spoke to the owner (whose name I can't remember, but it wasn't Kenny). I started in without thinking I needed to lead into it. I just told him I could reinforce his bathroom walls for a good price.

"Why the hell would I need that?" he asked me.

"For all the holes drunks punch in the wall," I said.

He looked at me real strange. "It happened once," he said. "Maybe, a long time ago, but it doesn't happen often enough for me to redo the whole bathroom."

I thanked him for his time and wondered how his bar was lucky enough to attract the peaceful drunks. So then I went to the Antler's Lounge, and then Old Joe's, and finally to Lucky's Corner, but I received the same response. They didn't have a problem with holes punched in the walls. So then I started to wonder how it was that Julio's bar attracted the aggressive drunks.

That night I went back to Zitios and got drunk myself. I went partly because I wanted to see if I needed to give the wall a second coat of paint. I also went because I was curious to see what the place was like on a Saturday night. I watched the bathroom door, which opened up to the dance floor—awkward placement if you ask me, because every time the door swung open you could see two dudes taking a piss. I sat at a table in the corner, just thinking and wondering, never taking my eyes off the bathroom door. I finally decided that I must look strange staring at the bathroom all night. People probably thought I liked looking at guys pissing. Who'd think I just cared about the drywall?

After a while, I had to take a piss. I stood in front of the urinal and stared at the freshly painted wall. I kept thinking to myself, *I have no desire whatsoever to punch my hand through the wall. Who does? Who stands here and thinks, "As soon as I'm done pissing I'm gonna punch a hole in this shit"?* And I couldn't figure it out. I thought that maybe if some guy were heartbroken he'd be upset enough, especially if he was liquored up on hard alcohol. But could there be that many heartbroken guys at this bar? There must be just as many at the other bars in town, but they weren't punching holes. I left the bathroom and went for another beer. I didn't need another one, but I also didn't want to go home. As I was waiting my turn, looking at the other people at the bar, something struck me that I hadn't considered before, and I hadn't considered it because it was so obvious: we were all Mexican. There were one or two white guys in the far room and a fat blonde girl with her tits hanging out at the bar, but other than that every face was brown. Was that the difference between this bar and the others? Is that why this one alone had holes in the bathroom? Were we all just a bunch of fucking machos with too much testosterone? I looked around. People were laughing, talking, drinking. Some played pool or darts, others danced. Most everyone looked happy. I looked for an angry face, a face ready to punch something. There were none. Maybe just not that night, I thought to myself. I drank my beer and left.

Two weeks later, Julio called again and said that someone had punched the wall again.

"They put a hole through the ⅝"?" I asked.

"Not a hole," he said, "but they smashed it good. Dumb fuck probably broke his hand on it, but the wall still looks bad. For now, just clean it up, but if it happens again we'll need something even stronger."

"I could put the studs closer together," I said. "But I'd have to tear everything out."

"Maybe later," he told me. "Like I said, just patch it up before tonight if you can and we'll see."

So I patched it up, and while I was working I thought of a plan. Not a good one, but I figured it was worth a try. This time I didn't paint it. I left a good coat of mud, a thick coat that wouldn't dry completely for at least a day. Then I went home, showered and changed, and went back to the bar. I sat in my corner, nursed a beer, and waited. But the longer I waited, the more I started thinking my plan was stupid. Before I had been thinking that if someone punched the wall, the wet mud would leave a trace on his hand. That's if he didn't notice and decide to wash it off, which I didn't think would happen. Somehow wall punching and hand washing didn't seem to go together. But then as the bar filled up, and the dance floor did as well, and the strobe light got going, I realized that from my corner I wouldn't be able to see the mud on someone even if he dumped his hands in a slosh bucket. So I left my seat and walked toward the bathroom. There was a barstool close to the bathroom door, but you had to be playing one of those electronic games to sit there. I decided it'd give me good cover. So I played poker, and then one where they had two photos side-by-side and you had to find what was different about each one, but I wasn't really paying attention. I was trying to listen over the DJ's bass and inspect the hands of everyone who left the bathroom. After about a half hour I heard a thump. There may have been others, but this one happened just as the song paused for a second before revving up again. I lunged for the bathroom door and opened it to find a guy staring at his knuckles, which were smeared with wet mud. I locked the door behind me.

"You punching the wall?" I asked. Maybe I should've been more careful, but I'm a big guy and can take care of myself. Plus, this kid didn't look tough. He looked up at me, not really able to focus on anything.

"What the fuck is this shit?" he asked, showing me his hands.

"That's joint compound, you idiot. Now what are you doing punching the wall?" I thought of telling him that I was going to throw him out or something, but I wasn't there as a bouncer. I repeated my question.

"What, this wall?" he asked.

"Yeah, that wall. Why are you punching it?"

"I didn't punch no wall!" he said, still staring at his hand.

"Yes, you did, that's why you got mud all over your knuckles."

Now he looked at the wall, as if it were something very strange and confusing. "Man, I don't even know what you're talking about," he said.

He was too drunk to get anything out of, but I did learn one thing. There were probably more people punching walls than the number of holes. I don't know why I hadn't thought about that, but it made sense. It's possible for a guy to punch hard enough to break through standard ½" drywall, but it'd be hard to punch an outright hole in the ⅝" drywall. Over the course of the night, though, after enough blows to weaken the wall, someone could come in and bust a hole with one punch. Anyway, I let the kid go, and by the time I went back to my stool someone was playing a game on the electronic screen. So I waited by the bathroom door, not caring if anyone wondered what the hell I was doing. I just listened. In the next few hours, I heard five more thumps, and each time I burst into the bathroom to confront the puncher, and each time it was denied, denied as though they truly didn't have any idea what I was talking about, even with the traces of mud on their knuckles. Finally, I got fed up. I wanted a reason, that was it. Just one reason why someone would punch a goddamn wall. I waited for another thump. And while I was waiting I watched the guys I had confronted earlier. Two of them watched me back. I glared at them. They seemed normal, and except for the first kid, none of them were too drunk. They weren't thugs either. They returned to kick it with friends or dance with girls. Only one of them posted up against the wall and looked like he wouldn't have minded more trouble.

Finally, I heard another thump, followed by an "Oh, shit!" This time the guy couldn't deny it. His hand was still stuck in the wall. He turned to me, his eyes wide with surprise. "Look at this!" he said. I locked the door behind me. "Yeah, look at it," I said. "Now, you wanna tell me why you punched it?" He removed his hand from the wall, opening and closing his fist. He'd hurt himself. "Damn," he said, "I didn't even punch it that hard."

"I don't care how hard you punched it, I just want to know why you did it."

"Did what?"

"Punched the wall?"

"What do you mean, *why* I punched the wall?"

"Exactly, fool. *Why,* standing *here,* did you decide to punch *that* wall?"

"Man, I don't know! I just did."

"You just did! Does that make any sense to you? After you take a piss, and before you wash your hands, you punch a wall? Now think about it, why did you punch the wall?"

"Man, let me go. Move out the way."

"No, because I'm the one who has to fix the drywall when drunk asses like you decide to act stupid. Now, either give me one reason why you punched it, or I'm gonna go to Julio right now and let him know that we've caught the dumbfuck who's caused him $500 in damage."

The guy sighed. If he was drunk before, he was sobering up now. He shrugged. "Man, I swear, I don't even know why I did it."

"Not good enough," I said.

He was quiet for a moment, and I could tell he was thinking. "I guess I was just taking a piss and, and, I don't know, I just felt, like, this feeling of being mad."

"At what? Mad at what? At your girlfriend, your dad, your friends? If you're mad, you gotta be mad at something."

"What are you, some kind of psychiatrist?"

"No, I just want an answer, damn it!"

"I can't give you one other than that. I wasn't mad at any-thing, man, I just wanted to punch something. That's it!"

Something told me that was all I was going to get. There was knocking on the door. "Let me in!" a voice cried. "Hurry up, I hella gotta take a piss!" I unlocked the door and let the fucker leave. I followed him out. The guy waiting to take a piss almost lunged past me, unbuckling his pants as he did so. As the bath-room door shut, I heard him say to no one but himself, "Damn, some fool punched a hole in this wall!" Then a few seconds later I heard another thump. That was when I learned there were copycats involved. No reason other than someone else did it before him.

That night I couldn't sleep. I was bothered by what had hap-pened. I knew the guy was telling the truth, and that if those other idiots had admitted to punching the wall they probably would have told me the same thing. They punched it because they were mad, but what they were mad at they probably couldn't say. I've always been even tempered. I get angry, but nothing ever bothers me enough to catch me off guard, make me react in a way I regret later. All my brothers have tempers, my dad too. Not bad, like you're always watching what you say because you don't want to end up in a fight. I do know guys like that. No, they're all good to their wives and kids and never hit them, so far as I know. But sometimes they just lash out, usu-ally over something really small, or at least it seems so at the time. I remember once my brother couldn't get the television

remote to work, and instead of getting new batteries or something, he just threw the remote at the television screen, breaking the remote and cracking the screen. Another time, my
oldest brother couldn't get cell-phone reception, and he just
threw the phone against the wall, smashing it to pieces. Both
times, everyone told them to calm down, but we never asked,
"Why did you do that? *Why*, think about it, why? That made no
sense, what you just did, no sense at all. Let's talk it out, damn
it." I guess you just assume some people got tempers, some people got things on their mind, things bothering them that take
hold all of a sudden, and asking why they threw the remote or
the cell phone was like asking them the meaning of life. Who
knows, that's just the way it is.

The next week I ripped apart the bathroom at Zitios Bar. I put
in studs every eight inches rather than every sixteen. And then
over the studs I put a metal sheet, and then over the metal sheet
I put in two panels of 5⁄8" drywall. You'd have had to have been
Mike Tyson to punch through this.

But I guess it didn't surprise me when several months later
Julio called me and told me that someone had damaged the wall.
"We caught him though," he said. "He admitted it too. He agreed
to pay for the damage. But it's not a hole, it's like a dent. Just put
some plaster over it, and it'll be fine." So that's what I did. I just
spackled the indentation, sanded it down, and then painted over
it. When I was done, I asked Julio what the guy's name was.

"Who?" Julio asked, as if he'd forgotten why I was there at
the bar in the first place.

"The guy who punched the wall."

"Oh. Cesar Trejo," he said.

"What is he, a boxer or something?" I asked.

He shook his head. "Nah, just pissed off at the world," Julio
said. "He was in Iraq. Came back fucked up."

"Is he big?" I asked. I pictured a giant.

"Stocky," Julio said. "Not that big though."

After that I forgot the name Cesar Trejo, but I did think a lot
about the dent, which wasn't really a dent at all. On close

184

inspection, you could see that it was the impression of the guy's knuckles. Like his signature, or like when people write their names in cement or carve their initials in a tree, a way of leaving your mark forever, or at least for a long time. And here I'd gone and patched it up, erased it. I told the guys at work about it. Told them about the double studs, the metal sheet, the two panels of ⅝" drywall. I told them about the knuckles. Most didn't believe me. Those who did thought that maybe it was the metal sheet that crumpled, rather than cracked, allowing for the impression. Most likely that's what happened. Either way, he'd hit it hard. I kept thinking how close I put the studs.

It was some time before I saw Julio again. I asked him about the bathroom walls at Zitios. He told me that he hadn't any problems since. I made some joke about not letting the guy who dented it back into the bar. He looked at me as if he didn't know what I was talking about.

"You know," I said, "the guy who left his damn knuckles in the wall."

The expression on his face changed. Now he remembered. That was when he told me that Cesar Trejo had killed himself.

II

I don't know why I went, or I do—I went because I couldn't stop thinking about the knuckles in the wall—but I don't know why I couldn't stop thinking about them. And I don't know how the idea entered my head that I would feel better if I found out who this Cesar Trejo guy was. Or not even feel better, but just forget the damned knuckles.

I asked Julio where Cesar's parents lived. I thought he'd ask me why, but he didn't. He just asked some other guy at the bar, and the guy drew me a map of how to get there. He could have just told me—it was across the tracks, two blocks down, and then over—but the guy was happy drunk and wanted to be helpful. It took us about five minutes just to find a pen, and after all that it barely worked on the napkin. The next day I went and found the place easy enough. There was a stained wood sign on the porch that said "The Trejos." I rang the doorbell and an older man with a graying mustache answered. "Mr. Trejo?" I asked. He didn't ask me what I wanted or anything, he just opened the door and invited me in. He told me he was just about to sit down for coffee and asked if I wanted some too. I said yes, and he called to his wife in the other room to make it. She came out a second later and asked how I liked my coffee. I told her with sugar and cream, and she set both in front of me, then she poured herself a cup and sat down at the table with us. It was only then that Cesar's father asked what they could do for me.

I didn't know where to begin, so I started with the truth, which was that I put up drywall for a living, and then I talked about the holes in the bathroom at my friend Julio's bar, and then I jumped to the part about the knuckles left in the wall and how I couldn't stop thinking about them. I was nervous for some reason and I knew that I was going on and on, but I couldn't stop myself, even when I started describing shit that didn't matter, like how I had reinforced the wall. Actually, Cesar's father was interested in that, and he even asked if I'd tried using plywood, and we could've easily kept going because he clearly liked talking construction, but then Cesar's mother started to cry.

"Why are you crying?" Mr. Trejo asked his wife.

Mrs. Trejo wiped her eyes with her apron and shook her head. "Nothing, it's just hard, sometimes, to see Cesar's friends and for Cesar not to be around."

I felt bad then. That's probably why they had invited me in. I hesitated, but told them anyway. "You know, I didn't actually know Cesar," I said.

"You didn't?" his father asked. "I thought you looked familiar. You've never been here before?"

"No, I haven't," I said.

He asked if I knew any of his other children. I told him I didn't.

Now he grew suspicious. I think if it had just been the two of us it wouldn't have mattered, but because his wife had started to cry it made the situation more awkward. His voice was less friendly now. "So then what do you want?"

"I want to know who it was who punched that wall so hard."

I think they thought I was still trying to find out who was at fault, and not that I was trying to learn more about the person who did it, because Mr. Trejo asked, "You want us to pay for damage that our dead son may or may not have committed months ago? Who even told you it was him?"

"No, no, that's not what I meant," I said quickly. "Cesar already paid for it to be fixed a long time ago, and I already fixed it. Like I said, I do drywall. I just wanted somehow, I guess, to learn more about Cesar. Like who he was, what kind of person. Because I can't stop thinking about, you know, his knuckles in the plaster."

They both looked at me like I was crazy. Mrs. Trejo started to cry again.

"He came back from Iraq very angry, very confused," Mr. Trejo said.

His parents gave me several names and numbers. Some were friends, others siblings. They also gave me Cesar's ex-girlfriend's number. They told me that she would be good to talk to. Her name was Marie. After talking to them, I felt bad, which I guess I should've expected—how else was I going to feel talking to parents about their dead son? I thought maybe I should stop this investigation (by now I'd started calling it that), but I still wanted to know more about Cesar. His mom and dad talked about him as if he were an angel. He'd gotten in trouble, sure, but what kid doesn't, they told me. It was Iraq that changed him. Everything before was heaven, everything after was hell. But parents are always going to have one view of their son, and usually that view is stuck somewhere in the fifth grade. So I knew that if I was ever going to let this thing go I was going have to talk to someone else. Maybe I should have called one of his brothers first. But that night I kept looking at the names and the phone numbers they'd given me, and Marie's name stood out from all the rest.

When she answered, her voice surprised me. It was chirpy, spunky—I don't know the word, bubbly maybe. I expected her to sound depressed. I thought maybe it'd even be hard to hear her because she would talk so low, barely above a whisper. So the cheerfulness caught me off guard, and as I explained the reason for my phone call I knew I wasn't making any sense. She kept saying, "Wait a second, *what?*" I did my best to describe the drywall and knuckle impression in the wall, but the truth is I don't know what I said. Finally, I shut up and Marie was quiet for a long time. Then she said, "I don't understand what you're talking about. You weren't friends, were you?"

"No," I said. "I didn't know him. Maybe it seems strange. Who can explain why certain things stick with you? I just need to know who those knuckles belonged to."

She was quiet on the other line, and I thought maybe she was thinking deeply about what I'd said, like I'd touched some nerve, but then I could hear her muffled voice telling someone to leave the room and that she would be out in a minute. Finally she asked, "Uh, do you want to meet me for a drink or something?"

I didn't know what to say. The truth is, I liked her voice. I was curious to know what she looked like. It had even crossed my mind that it'd be nice to meet this girl. But I didn't think she would come right out and ask me if I wanted to grab a drink. I decided it was fine. I had called to talk to her, and it might as well be in person.

We met at Julio's bar. She was tiny, probably not even five foot. Her black hair was pulled back tight, and she had mousy ears. She had this strange smile on her face, like we were doing something we shouldn't be doing. We talked for a little while about random things. Nothing I remember. We got our drinks and then, without me even asking, she started talking. Her voice didn't change, it stayed cheerful, like she was talking about her plans for the weekend or something. "Right after Cesar got home, I went to his house and spoke to his mom," she said. "She told me he hadn't left his room for three days straight. She thought maybe I could help. And so I walked with her to Cesar's room, and she whispered loudly, 'May God Bless you, you are the best thing that ever happened to him.' Made me feel guilty. No one knew we had broken up before his last tour. She knocked on the door and we waited, but nothing. So his mother said through the door, 'It's Marie.' And still nothing. So I say, 'It's me, Cesar.' And he says, 'I don't want to talk to that bitch,' just like that. I remember his mom moaned and covered her face with her apron. I just placed my arm around her, and she kept saying sorry over and over. She couldn't understand what had happened to him. I told her that he would be fine, he just needed time, and I think this made her feel better, but I don't think I believed it myself."

"Why?" I asked.

"Look, I'll show you something—" she pulled out a shiny pink book from her purse—"He'd already taken off, but he was still in the country. So one night, I shut off my phone for some reason, and I missed his text messages. When I woke up in the morning there were nineteen of them waiting for me. I wrote them in this diary thing I keep, I don't even know why I wrote them down. I guess so that I wouldn't forget how scared they made me feel. I loved him, I missed him, I wanted to be with him—we'd been together since we were fifteen—but I couldn't be with him. Here," she said, handing me the book, "I don't even want to look at the page."

I read them. They were the text messages of a crazed man. Or maybe just a heartbroken kid. A lot of *fuck u*'s and *bitch*es and accusations, followed by apologies. I'd texted messages like those before, just not nineteen of them. The only one that stuck with me was the last. He wrote, "Just tell me ur happy without me and Ill leave u alone forever."

"I sent one text message back," Marie said. "I just said, 'I love you. You're my best friend. But I'm afraid of you,' and that was it."

We were quiet for a minute, and then Marie asked me, "Tell me again, why do you want to know all this about Cesar?"

I was looking at my beer. At the shiny pink book in front of me. At Sammy behind the bar. I was trying to look at anything but Marie. Finally, I turned to her, and she was staring right at me, like she'd been looking at the side of my face the entire time. I shrugged my shoulders, but I didn't say anything. I don't think I knew why I was doing this anymore. She kept looking at me, and I kept looking at her. She looked sad now, but I didn't think she was sad about Cesar. Maybe it's just what I wanted to think. She turned her legs toward me. Our stools were close together. I placed my hand on her leg. I don't even know why.

That night Marie came back to my apartment. We drank some more. She asked me if I had any weed. I told her I did and we smoked some. Then we had sex. We finished and she got up, and without putting on any clothes she went to the bathroom. I heard her raise the lid of the toilet. Then she started to pee, and for some reason, listening to the trickle of her piss hit the water, I realized what I'd done and I didn't feel good about it. Until that moment she hadn't really existed. Like it had all been some dream, some drunken hookup forgotten the next day. But what I'd done and what I didn't feel good about, I didn't exactly know. I had met up with a pretty girl, and one thing led to another—that's what had happened. Maybe it was what led up to it that bothered me. How'd I go from investigating holes in the wall to this? When she came out of the bathroom, the light hit my face and she must have noticed that something was wrong. She asked if I was okay. I told her yeah, but I don't think she believed me. After a long silence, she asked, "How'd we end up here?"

"I know," I said. "I was asking myself the same thing."

"You know who you should talk to?" she said. "His brother, Freddy. They were living together when Cesar's parents kicked him out of the house. I heard that right before Cesar killed himself, he pointed the gun at Freddy's head and made him get down on his knees and beg for his life. So Freddy did, and then Cesar asked him if he really thought he'd shoot his own brother. And Freddy couldn't answer, because he was sobbing so hard.

190

Finally, Cesar went into his room, and that was when Freddy heard the gun go off . . ."

"Crazy," I said, but I'd stopped listening. I didn't want to think about Cesar Trejo anymore. I just wanted to fall asleep and for the morning to come and for Marie to leave.

"Yeah, crazy," she said sleepily. She yawned and then kissed me and placed her warm body against mine. She quickly fell asleep in my arms. She was on top of me. I couldn't believe how tiny she was. Her breath was warm and light, and she was like a little kid sleeping. I couldn't sleep though. I kept staring at the ceiling, hoping my eyes would get heavy, but just when they would and I started to lose myself I would become aware that I had Cesar Trejo's ex-girlfriend naked on top of me. I imagined if I were him, what I would do to me . . . if I were him. I didn't know anything about Iraq or what had happened over there. I just knew that he had loved Marie, this girl in my arms, and he'd loved her and he'd lost her, and I had found her. That was all I knew about Cesar Trejo. That and his knuckles. I imagined us alone in the bathroom of Julio's bar, and instead of punching the reinforced wall, he was punching me, breaking my nose, my jaw, blood everywhere, my face no longer my face, my flesh just wet mud absorbing his knuckles over and over.